BATTLE EARTH III

NICK S. THOMAS

© 2012 Nick S. Thomas

The right of Nick S. Thomas to be identified as the Author
of the Work has been asserted by him in accordance with the
Copyright, Designs and Patents Act 1988.

First published in the United Kingdom in Feb 2012
by Swordworks Books.

All rights reserved. No part of this publication may be
produced, stored in a retrieval system, or transmitted in
any form or by any means, without the prior permission in
writing of the publisher, nor be otherwise circulated in any
form of binding or cover other than in which it is published
and without a similar condition including this condition
being imposed on the subsequent purchaser.

All characters in this publication are fictitious and any
resemblance to real persons, living or dead, is purely
coincidental.

ISBN 978-1-906512-96-5

Typeset by Swordworks Books
Printed and bound in the UK & US
A catalogue record of this book is available
from the British Library

Cover design by Swordworks Books
www.swordworks.co.uk

BATTLE EARTH III

NICK S. THOMAS

PROLOGUE

The Earth War had raged for two months, but humanity had lost more in the first week than a year of any previous conflict. The Ares research base on Mars had been the first target. The Lunar colony, the only other substantial human colony outside of Earth's atmosphere had been next. The survivors of the five hundred thousand moon colonists had fled below ground to continue to wage a guerrilla war.

The alien invaders had deployed a base in the Atlantic that had expanded to the size of many countries. Spain and North Africa had quickly fallen. France had been the bastion of Europe, but now lay in ruins. Major Taylor remains on light duty to recover from his injuries. The United States fights at its shoreline, and South America is on the brink of falling. Soldiers from all around the globe fight alongside one another to save their planet.

Major Taylor's heroic and successful sabotaging of the enemy super weapon at the town of Poitiers had kept the human race in the fight, but him out of it. The marine officer still lay recovering from his injuries as his comrades struggled on. At Ramstein, on the western edge of Germany, the armies of Earth and of the Krycenaean invaders continue to battle through a bitter stalemate.

CHAPTER ONE

"Shhh," whispered Chandra.

She looked back to the road through the thick foliage she was taking cover in. A small enemy column approached in the narrow road at the base of the valley. She lifted her Mappad to check their location. They were five kilometres west of Ramstein; exactly where they should be. She looked down at the exoskeleton suit which was strapped to her body and the huge weapon she bore in her one hand; the weight being of little notice. Come on you bastards, she thought.

Across the roadway she could just make out Captain Friday's position. He was poised and ready for the onslaught they all eagerly awaited. They outnumbered the enemy three to one and had plenty of Reiter's new hardware. She took slow deep breaths to calm her nerves. As she breathed out, vapour rose from her mouth. They were rapidly approaching a cold winter, and it was a crisp morning.

The Company had been waiting in ambush since before dawn. Other than the approaching vehicles, the valley was quiet. Even the burning smell of the ruined cities of the country was absent from the tranquil countryside on the border; and the bitter coldness, of being immobile on an autumn morning, was only overcome by the rush of adrenaline from knowing they were about to fight.

Three enemy armoured vehicles approached along the road with over a dozen Mechs visible on top of each of them. They were clearly some form of open top armoured personnel carrier. They cruised along the road at a solid and steady pace, but without any form of urgency; just weeks before, the enemy armour was a frightful sight to the infantry. Come on, Chandra thought.

She licked her lips as they approached, and she envisaged their vehicles burning and Mechs scattered dead across the roadway. It was a brutal thing to wish for. She only accepted the desire in the knowledge that it was them or her. She felt no empathy for the creatures. The Major could only imagine what it must be like to have to face humans in such a conflict. Her hatred ran as deep as the soldiers of the most extreme religious wars in their planet's history.

The Major stared intently at the approaching force, and she didn't look back at her comrades again. She knew they had her back. The enemy below were oblivious to their position. Their forces were well concealed within the evergreens of the valley. She could feel the excitement inside her grow as she lifted her weapon into view and readied herself to scream her battle cry.

Her mouth was dry now. The build up of tension had caused her to forget to breathe as she looked down the sight of her weapon. She coughed lightly and took in one last deep breath to be able to bellow the only command she needed.

"Fire!" she cried.

Before she could squeeze the trigger of her weapon, a hail of gunfire rang out. Pulses of light emanated from the tree line as Reiter's latest weapons rained death upon the invaders. Chandra had been lucky enough to be able to hang onto all of the latest equipment for her Company. Rifle and grenade fire joined the shooting gallery as the volley smashed the enemy vehicles.

Chandra watched as the Mechs tried to leap off the vehicles and out of the line of brutal fire. Many were struck and killed outright before they could get to their feet. She watched in amazement as the creatures were torn apart by their fire. It was a turkey shoot that only made her believe for the first time in weeks that they had a chance. She revelled in the destruction as she continued to fire relentlessly.

The almost continuous hail of gunfire began to die

down as Mechs tumbled to the hard mud beside the road, and others slumped lifelessly atop their vehicles. The Major got to her feet and admired the results of their work. Smoke arose from one of the vehicles, and steam poured out from the charred wounds of the Mechs.

Chandra had become accustomed to seeing the sight of dead soldiers, and it always made her feel sick, but not Mechs. She could not see them as people. They were not their equals, and they had no value. Their thick blue blood that seeped out through the gaping holes in their armour was no different to seeing oil leak from a car for the battle-hardened Major.

The valley went silent once again as the Company awaited the Major's orders. They're nothing, she thought, and no better than us. We can beat these bastards. Chandra knew the war was far from over, but she was starting to gain some hope of victory. Taylor's heroic deeds had shown the strength that was left in the human race. She turned and looked to the section beside her, nodding for them to follow her as she waved them forward with her weapon.

The Reitech exoskeleton suits, as they had become to be know after their designer, proved their worth every day. The first few useable suits had been delivered to Brigadier Dupont's command, but they were still far from a common sight among the human armies. Chandra found the equipment to fit like a glove. Ever concentrating on their enemy, she barely noticed its presence anymore.

She stepped cautiously down the embankment to the carnage below. The stabilisation of the suit kept her balance perfectly on the uneasy terrain, as others slipped and slid on the slope. She reached even ground and stepped over the bloodied body of one of the creatures. Smoke arose from the burning hole in its armour.

Chandra walked past one of the vehicles, but there was no sign of life. She could already hear her troops ripping the cab open to be sure as she moved on to the next. As she approached, a door to the front of the vehicle swung out and smashed into her weapon. The force ripped it out of her hands and broke the sling hook holding it to her side. Her back crashed into the hard hull of the vehicle. Her armour took the impact, but the wind was taken out of her.

A tall creature climbed out and stood before her. The beast towered over the short officer who, with a frame so slight, appeared as a child before the monster. It studied her for just a moment before rushing at her like a charging bull. Its sudden turn of speed caught her off guard, but she still managed to narrowly avoid its strike.

The monster crashed into the side of the vehicle with the loud resonating clash of metal on metal. It wore a skin-tight suit that was of much smaller and less bulky proportions than they had been used to seeing the creatures in. It appeared to offer only minimal protection.

From her hunched position, the Major thrust up with the power of her body, and aided by her suit and with all she could muster, delivered an uppercut into the creature's stomach.

The Reitech suit afforded her a strength she had never known. Her hardened kneecap drove hard into the creature, causing it to fold at the waist. Before she could make a second strike, the beast swung wildly with a powerful hook. She ducked under the strike and spun around the beast. As she lifted back up to a standing position, she drew her knife and thrust it up under the beast's jaw.

Thick warm blood gushed down over her hand. If she had closed her eyes, she could not have told the difference between their blood and her own. The beast spun in anger and struck her with the back of its hand. The strike felt as if it almost broke her neck and threw her onto her back. She looked up from the ground as the creature took a few wobbly steps towards her. It finally collapsed onto the hard and cold ground beside her.

"Major!" shouted Monty.

The soldier rushed to her side with his brother close behind. He outstretched his hand and hauled her to feet. Blood gushed from her nose and trickled out from her mouth. She saw Monty looking at the wound and instinctively drew her hand across her face, looking down at the smear of blood on her skin. The blood tasted sour in the cold morning, and worse than it normally would.

"Jesus, Major, that's some hard core shit," exclaimed Blinker.

Captain Friday arrived beside her and looked down at the body of the creature with the Major's knife still imbedded up to its hilt under the jaw. He looked up at the Major to investigate her injuries.

"You ok?" he asked.

She nodded. Chandra was still in shock from the attack. Her instincts and muscle memory had taken over her actions to save her life, but now she was starting to realise how close she had come to death.

"Thank God he didn't have armour."

Chandra nodded in agreement.

"Every time they get close to our troops, they rip us apart. These new suits have given us a lot more strength, but we need weapons that can handle hand-to-hand combat."

"Shit, you really want to do that again, Ma'am?" snapped Blinker.

She quickly turned around to oppose the Private. The blood on her face had already begun to congeal in the cold morning chill. She could never stand tall over any of the men, but her presence was enough to command respect.

"Uhh... sorry, Ma'am."

"No, you're right. I wouldn't want to do it again, and certainly not against one of the fully armoured bastards. But were it a choice, we wouldn't fight them at all! Fact is we have to do whatever we need to. The next time we get into hand-to-hand, I want to be prepared."

"Guess we better get on to Reiter," mused Friday.

"He's probably thought of it before us, Captain. Let's see what he has to offer. Do a last sweep of the site, and be sure none of them live. We move out in five."

They were on foot to return to base. Vehicle patrols to the west of Ramstein attracted too much attention from enemy air and artillery support. Neither side had launched any noteworthy offensives since the destruction of their facility in Poitiers. Chandra thought to herself as she peered around the valley. They're in disarray. For once they aren't moving forward. We could break them here.

The return to Ramstein was without incident. They passed four other allied units, and each one of them from another nation. Was this what we needed? Chandra asked herself; a common enemy to ally the Earth's people together for the first time in its history. Then she remembered the loss of Charlie Jones and the Frenchman behind it, Legrant. The Mayor of Amiens, where they had been betrayed. She still harboured a bitter hatred for the man and prayed to never see him again, for she didn't know if she would be able to restrain herself.

As the Company approached the western Perimeter of Ramstein, they could all make out the outline of Taylor waiting for them in front of the trenches. Behind him lay dozens of armoured vehicles and many more troops. His crutch had gone. His injuries had healed quickly, but he still showed the scars of the beating that Karadag had given him. The marine Major was smiling as they drew near.

"Good to see you back with us!" shouted Chandra.

She strode up to Mitch until she was close enough to speak privately.

"You cleared to come back?" she whispered.

"I figure so."

"You figure?"

Taylor's smile grew wider.

"I wouldn't miss this for the world."

"Without you there might not have been one," she replied.

"You trying to kiss ass, Major?" he jested.

The two of them laughed as they turned and led the Company through the defences and into the safety of the base. It was already a hive of activity. Just a few weeks earlier, they had rushed across abandoned and desolate districts of the base to reach the western perimeter. Now it was littered with military vehicles and soldiers.

Ramstein was no longer an Air Force base. Its airfields had been lined with armoured vehicles. For the first time in decades, the base was truly alive. The hangars were over spilling with troops using them for accommodation. Tens of thousands of troops now occupied the base which was previously just a few years from closure.

"General Schulz still making you work at HQ?" asked Chandra.

"Just as an advisor. You know things have run a hell of a lot smoother since he took command."

She nodded in agreement.

"Dupont still bitter about it?"

"Of course."

"Well, we're on German soil now, so it's only right and proper they oversee the defence."

"Commander Phillips is also still on board and assisting, along with leaders from most nations around here that I can think to name. A day with them could never be described as fun, but it is interesting."

"Whoever thought it could work?" she asked. "The military minds of all nations coming together in a joint cause?"

"It isn't all plain sailing. Dupont is still bitter, and rightly so. He has lost his country and many of his people."

Chandra stopped and turned back to look at her Company. The troops came to a halt without command. They looked weary. The war had been reduced to a slog over the western border of Germany with no significant progress for either side. It was a meat grinder. They knew the brass would think that a good thing. All intelligence would suggest that the human forces significantly outnumbered the enemy, so much so that they could afford like-for-like losses.

"Good work! We kicked some arse today! Get some chow. At 1500 hours we take over guard duty at the western gate. Until then your time is your own!"

A restrained cheer rang out. It was a relief to the troops to be given a rest, but none of them were under any illusions concerning their situation. Captain Friday paced up to join the two Majors.

"We got any news on re-enforcements?" he asked. "We need to get back some way to battalion strength if we're going to stay effective."

"We've got no such luck, Captain. UK forces are amassed, but I have little idea on their intentions. You won't be seeing any more yanks this side of the Atlantic anytime soon. Word is your boys are having a rough time of it."

"Any news on that front?"

Taylor turned to his friend with a grim expression.

"The invasion has been widespread across the coast. As far as I can tell, New York has been hammered. Maine, Phili, Massachusetts and Delaware are mostly under enemy control. Most of the fighting right now is happening in Pennsylvania and Virginia."

"How about DC?"

"Last I heard there were a couple of divisions fighting it out there. God knows how long they can keep it up."

Friday sighed. The thought of such vast warfare on their own soil was something they could barely comprehend.

BATTLE EARTH III

Chandra stepped forward and patted him on the shoulder.

"Don't worry about it, Captain. Invasion is nothing new to the rest of us. The game isn't over."

Friday still shook his head in disbelief.

"We should be there," he muttered.

"No," snapped Taylor. "We should be wherever the fight is, and that's exactly what we're doing."

"Major!"

Chandra spun around. Her hand reached for the weapon slung on her side as her pulse raced. She had become accustomed to being on guard at all times. Lieutenant Green stood before her.

"What is it?" she snapped.

"Commander Phillips is requesting your presence, along with Major Taylor."

"Got it, thank you, Lieutenant. That'll be all."

Green rushed off to join the rest of the Company and to enjoy the few hours of recuperation they would get.

"What do you think he wants?" asked Taylor.

"You know better than me. You're the one that's been on base."

"Not a clue. Hopefully he has some news."

Chandra turned to Friday.

"You can join us also, Captain."

"You sure the Commander will be keen on that idea?"

"I don't give a shit. We've lost more soldiers than I want to remember. The fact that we three are still alive is a miracle in itself. There may come a time when you have to take over from Taylor or myself. I'd rather you were ready for that responsibility."

"She's right," mused Taylor.

"Not the most positive of thoughts, Ma'am," went on Friday.

"We have to be realistic, Captain. We have made it this far, and I pray we all make it through this, but we must be prepared for the worst."

The Captain agreed, even if he didn't like the thought of it. The three of them turned and continued on towards Headquarters. Troops from a dozen different nations saluted and greeted them as they passed down the busy roads. Chandra's Company no longer had any vehicles at their disposal, not even for the Major herself. They scrounged lifts where they could.

"Rains still in the area?" asked Chandra.

"Yeah, he's running high priority jobs for command. I saw him a few hours back."

As they reached an intersection, they halted abruptly to avoid being run down by a dozen Russian heavy tanks rolling across the thoroughfare. The three officers could barely hear each other over the constant noise of chatter and vehicles travelling throughout the base. Combat-weary soldiers lay about, getting any rest they could. Fresh recruits sat awaiting deployment, and there was no excitement or enthusiasm in their eyes. They had seen the faces of those who had faced the Mechs and the ever-mounting dead.

Many of the troops looked at the Reitech suits with amazement and envy. There were still less than two hundred on the base. Production had been marred by delays due to the chaos that had engulfed the planet. Transportation networks were in shambles, and many nations' workforces were in disarray.

Few begrudged the Company's almost exclusive issue of the latest equipment, and anyone who did, was quickly reminded of their heroic actions from the day the war began. Chandra and Taylor were becoming household names among the human armies along with their battalion; the Inter-Allied had become known to many, as the 'Immortals'.

Few knew of the horrific losses of the unit. Soldiers had become familiar with the stories of their dare devil escapades and were never informed of the heavy price which they had paid for such antics. They only saw the triumphant returns and celebrated their victories.

Up ahead, they could see Phillips sat on top of a freight box with a mug of tea in his hand. His uniform was as clean as the newest recruits. There was no dread in his face. He had not met the enemy face to face, and to him the Mechs were nothing more than a statistic. Just as the human dead were a number on a computer.

"You can bet your ass he took the credit for your

mission to Poitiers," said Friday.

Taylor was amused by Friday's vocalisation recently. He had always been a man of few words. Maybe he just never had much that was important enough to voice an opinion, thought Taylor. The war had put many of their troubles into perspective. The petty squabbles in their lives seemed to be exactly that.

"Undoubtedly," replied Chandra. "But had it gone wrong, it would have been his balls."

"You think that responsibility is equal to the risks we take with our lives?" asked Taylor.

"No, but we must each play a part."

The Commander lifted his mug as a greeting to them when he saw them approach. He had a smile on his freshly washed face, as if they were back home and enjoying a relaxing weekend. Deep down they all knew the pressure upon the Commander, and the work that he put in, but they could not help but feel he hadn't earned his reputation in combat.

"Got any news for us, Sir?" shouted Chandra.

Phillips got to his feet and waved for them to follow him into the building he was sat in front of. They walked through and into a large mirrored elevator that took them fifty metres below the surface where the underground HQ had been established. The doors opened, and Phillips strode out without a word.

Just as the Commander was about to reach the pair of

guards stood either side of the Command centre entrance, he veered off down a side corridor, leading the three officers into a smaller meeting room. He slumped down into a chair in the room as they went in behind him.

"Shut the door."

Friday begrudgingly closed the door behind them. He didn't like being treated like a ranker, but there was little that could be said on the subject. Phillips looked up to see the three officers stood awaiting some big news. In that moment, his relaxed mood dropped as he realised quite how imposing the troops were in their Reitech suits. Only Taylor wore no armour, but he still carried a rifle and sidearm.

"What have you got for us, Sir?" asked Chandra.

"I have it on good authority that British forces are planning to cross the channel and engage the enemy in northern France. I don't know when, but the fact remains, that they will not do it until they can see we have brought the enemy to a halt."

"Well hell, Sir, we did that last week, didn't you hear?" fumed Taylor.

"I hear you, Major. I am doing everything in my power to convince Field Marshall Copley to launch his attack immediately. We have stopped the enemy once, but they were hot on our tails. We all know too well that we can't get the equipment we need to the frontline fast enough."

"And if we don't get all the support we need, there may

not be anyone left to use it," snapped Chandra.

Phillips nodded in agreement.

"I completely agree. I believe help is imminent. A British offensive in the north could be a game changer."

"How big an offensive are we talking, Sir?" asked Taylor.

"His Majesty's armies are fully prepared and ready for war. I have seen reports that Commonwealth forces have flocked to Britain to give assistance. If the British army is landing in France, they're doing so in number."

"Alright," muttered Friday.

"What about the US, Sir, any news?" asked Taylor.

"Not much beyond what you already know. They're having a hard time of it just as we are, but they are holding. Major, you have been key in the testing of Mr Reiter's research, and I am sure you have plenty more to give. These Reitech suits are now out of his hands. Find out what he's working on, and give what assistance you can."

"But I am cleared to return to the Company, Sir."

"We both know that isn't true, Major. There may come a time when we put wounded men out in the field to fight, but they will be desperate times indeed."

"Are things not already desperate enough?" asked Chandra.

"Look around. The base has been heavily reinforced. The Company is managing perfectly well. There is more to winning this war than being on the frontline."

Friday smirked in the background. He knew what the

Commander was saying. The frustration and pressure of being behind the lines whilst everyone he knew was in danger was not pleasant. So maybe it did take balls to do his job, thought Friday.

"Right now, we need every advantage we can get. Major, you're up for guard duty this afternoon, is that correct?"

"Yes, Sir. Light duties to give the troops a little rest," she replied.

"Good, then they can manage without you. Captain Friday will handle that while you assist Taylor. Your continued combat experience while he has been recovering should be valuable."

Chandra moved to confront the command, but Phillips interrupted her.

"Major, you two have more combined experience in close combat with this enemy than anyone I can think of. You'll be back to the front line before long. Any work you put in now could save just as many lives as you being out there."

Both of them knew there was no sense in arguing any further. The more Chandra thought about it, the more she had problems she wanted solutions for. She knew Reiter was the man for the job.

"We'll get on it, Sir."

"Good. Your Company is on base duty until further notice while you work on R&D."

The three officers saluted the Commander and quickly

turned and left. None of them spoke until they had got out of the building and once more into daylight and fresh air.

"Captain, we may well have a couple of days rest here. Giving us guard duty was just a simple way of getting our people out of any hard work, and they've earned it. We've got plenty more numbers than are needed for the area we have been posted. Be sure to get some e-readers and music up there. There are also beds that you can use on rotation."

"Yes, Ma'am."

"This is a rare chance for the Company to recuperate, so use it well."

Friday nodded as he turned and strode quickly back towards the Company who lay scattered about at a staging ground.

"I am guessing that nose wasn't busted in a fall?" asked Taylor.

Chandra smiled. It was one of the many near-death experiences she had faced of late. Having survived it, she could now look back on it with humour and analyse it further.

"Those things are deadly up close. I was lucky."

"Then clearly we have an agenda for Reiter."

* * *

Reiter sat in his office chair with his back to them. He stared out of the tall pane of glass that looked onto his research centre. A few employees worked casually in the room, but it was the quietest Taylor had ever seen it. The two officers could only see the scientist's mostly baldhead. A small grey patch of hair was all that remained of his hair. Even though they could not see his face, they could both tell he was frowning.

"Sir? You okay?" asked Chandra.

He swivelled round in his chair and glared at the Major.

"I hold no rank here. You are the officer. You can call me Doctor Reiter, or by my first name, if you would consider us close."

"What's going on here, Doc? Production is delayed, and we need the kit. Why's this place so quiet?"

"Manufacturing is out of our hands. We've been ordered to move on with further development of new ideas."

"Well, why aren't you?"

Reiter sighed at the insult.

"Mr Taylor. I have not stopped working my entire life. But without the resources and manpower I need, there is little more I can do."

"What do you mean?" asked Chandra.

"Most of my staff has been re-assigned to manufacturing plants to oversee the production of the equipment I designed. I am getting few deliveries of the supplies and resources I need. There isn't a lot I can do."

Taylor sighed and paced around the room.

"I am sure this has all been necessary, Doc. The only thing that matters right now is getting that hardware into combat."

Reiter nodded.

"Then why are you here?"

Taylor shook his head. He realised that he was asking just the opposite of the wise scientist.

"Command wants us to oversee your future developments."

Reiter coughed. He was in part amused and insulted at the same time.

"I appreciate the problems you are dealing with," said Chandra. "But you have to understand, we all face the same hardship. Our Company isn't getting the replacements we need. We aren't getting the support we need. Times are tough, and we have to manage."

Reiter nodded. He knew what the Major was saying was right before she'd said it, but he couldn't help but feel sidelined.

"I can't believe you've got nothing new on the drawing board?" asked Taylor.

Reiter swivelled around in his chair once again and smiled, as he looked out into his facility with his back to the two officers. Taylor squinted to look at a large item that two of the staff were lifting up onto a table. It appeared to be of a similar construction to the armour of the Reitech suits, but in a large rectangular sheet with grips on one side and a small window. He stepped around the scientist's desk to get a closer look but could not identify what he was looking at. He turned quickly to ask a question of Reiter but was interrupted.

"I am still working with what I have, Major."

The scientist smiled. Chandra stepped around to join the other two and marvel at the object. She already knew it would be a fascinating creation, but she just didn't know its purpose yet. Taylor couldn't wait any longer.

"What the hell is it?" he insisted.

Reiter gestured towards the suit Chandra was still wearing from her mission.

"The armour on the suits which you are wearing has proven successful, yes?"

"Damn right. It has saved more than a few lives."

"But its coverage is still limited. A suit of such armour would weigh more than double what the exoskeleton could hope to manage. That doesn't even take into account the problems of joints and other such weaknesses."

"Then what?" Taylor asked.

"My dear, Major, we do what fighting men have done for centuries. Carry a shield!"

Mitch looked into the lab with a dumbfounded expression. A shield was something utterly quaint and antiquated to his mind. He turned back around with the same shocked look.

"You're not serious?"

"I most certainly am, Major. The shield has throughout history proven to be the simplest, cheapest and most effective protection, when all things are considered. It provides the most coverage for its weight. It can be manufactured quickly and repaired just as easily."

"Then why aren't we using them already?"

"Look at the thing," exclaimed Chandra. "Those two techs are struggling to move it."

"Indeed. A shield that can withstand such high ballistic and thermal conditions will weigh eighty kilos or more, and a weight that will present no problem to the wearer of that suit."

He pointed to Chandra's equipment with pride.

"Come on, let's take a look."

Moments later, they stood before the huge slab shield which lay on top of the table. The construction was crude with huge visible bolt threads and a handle that looked as if it had come off a truck.

"We have salvaged what parts we could for this project. Things are a bit short, right now."

Taylor stepped up beside the shield and passed his hand over the metalwork. It felt cold and dull, just like the armour they wore with a slightly rough mottled texture. The composite material had remained a secret ever since it had been fitted to armoured vehicles two decades before. He slipped his fingers beneath it and attempted to lift.

Mitch's face strained as his muscles tensed, and the shield didn't move.

He placed his other hand alongside his first and put some effort in, lifting the shield edge from the table before dropping it clumsily back down onto the table. The vast shield landed with a crash that made the scientists cringe.

"Jesus, this thing weighs a tonne!"

Taylor took a step back and shook his head in astonishment at the creation.

"You think our suits can handle this?"

Reiter turned to Chandra and gestured for her to try. She stepped forward uncomfortably under the scrutiny of the pessimistic Taylor. She circled the table as she intently studied the device. It was so simple, and yet to her it was utterly alien. The Major reached forward, placed her hand on the grip of the shield and lifted.

Taylor gasped as Chandra lifted the device as if it were a bottle of water. She twisted it in to a comfortable grip as she moved it around and studied its coverage. The viewing window was made from inch thick ballistic plastic, affording at least some visibility. She turned head on to Taylor and hunched down behind the shield to allow him a view of its defensive ability.

"With this device, you will achieve at least ninety percent frontal protective coverage. You will be able to cover open ground in safety and fight where no cover exists," claimed Reiter.

Taylor nodded in astonishment at the facts he was being told. He was already starting to appreciate the potential for Reiter's device. It was in so many ways simple, and yet a beautifully efficient solution to their problem.

"With these shields, you will become the medieval knights of the modern era. You will be able to advance like armoured vehicles and move like infantry."

Taylor stepped up to Chandra, who stood with the shield in a guard position as if it weighed nothing at all.

"No strain at all? You can keep that up?" he asked.

Chandra squinted at him, trying to understand if he was picking on her for being a woman, or if he was just being serious.

"Barely notice it, nothing worse than carrying a rifle."

Taylor looked down at the launcher resting at her side.

"Pick it up, your weapon."

Chandra reached for the grip with her right hand, and then hesitated as she realised she didn't have her other arm to use with it. The Major lifted the weapon clumsily against the shield, trying to find a way to aim it from the protection of the shield.

"Ah, yes, you have found the next dilemma."

Taylor spun around on the spot with a furious expression.

"Dilemma? What good is the shield if we can't use our weapons?"

"I will remind you, Major, that this is an experimental

department. We develop solutions to problems. We have found a solution to the armour problem, and we will take it from there."

Taylor shook his head. God damn it, we haven't got time to waste on shit that won't work, he thought.

"I know your frustrations, Major, but this is life in research and development. I already have a few ideas on how to solve this problem. I just need a little time."

"Time? Shit, Doc, that's the one thing we definitely haven't got."

"Mitch!" shouted Chandra.

The marine officer turned at the call of his superior. She glared at him, and he instantly knew it was his cue to back down. He took a deep breath and turned back to the scientist.

"I'm sorry, but these aren't easy times for any of us. Your equipment has been saving lives, and that's making a big difference. I can see technology here that could be a real game changer, but you have to work faster."

"Then I beg that you convince your leaders to allocate more resources and manpower to my operations."

Chandra placed the shield down on the table beside her and pulled the Doctor around gently from his shoulder.

"Listen, I can see what you are doing here, and we desperately need everything you have to offer. If resources and manpower are what you need, then we will see it done."

The scientist nodded gratefully.

"Thank you, truly. You have all given me the greatest opportunities to develop my work here."

"No, Doc, thank you."

She turned back to Taylor.

"Let's get this man what he needs!"

CHAPTER TWO

The two officers headed towards the HQ building. They were intent on getting Reiter everything he needed to pursue his development of the equipment they had seen. As they passed two soldiers, Taylor caught an ear full of their conversation. The two men were from different nations and so were communicating in English.

"They aren't going to take me for whatever shit they are doing with humans. Why would they want prisoners anyway?"

"To study us, I guess," replied the other.

Taylor turned and rushed back to them. Chandra casually followed suit. She had not heard the conversation and was surprised at Mitch's sudden distraction. As she moved closer, she could hear the urgent questions he was asking.

"How do you know they're taking humans?"

"My brother saw it during his last mission. He's a pilot, and he said they were transporting prisoners west from Saarbrucken."

"You sure? You're sure they were alive?"

"Positive, Sir. He said they were mostly soldiers. Some were wounded, but they all looked alive."

"Alright, thanks."

Taylor turned back to Chandra and let the two soldiers continue on their way.

"You know what this means?"

"Let's not jump to any conclusions here," replied Chandra.

"Jones is alive, and you know it. I'd bet good money he is wherever those prisoners were being taken."

Taylor lifted a pocket on his combats and pulled out his Mappad. Seconds later, he had the map of the area and zoomed in to the city of Saarbrucken.

"We know Saarbrucken has become a major enemy staging point."

He tracked west along the main highway.

"There, Metz. It's the obvious place to hold prisoners. Far enough away from the front line but with easy access."

"That's a whole lot of maybes," mused Chandra.

"Come on, this is Jones we are talking about. We can't just leave him to die!"

Chandra shook her head. She knew that she should never entertain such an idea, but her feelings for Jones had clouded her judgement. She wanted him back just as much as Taylor, maybe more so. She lowered her head as she thought over the situation, until finally she looked back up to Mitch. It was clear he was not going to let it go, and she prayed that Jones was alive as they hoped.

"Even if he is alive and imprisoned, what are we going to do about it?"

"We've pulled off far greater tasks. If we can get some intel on his location, then we have the equipment and troops ready to get him out."

"Schulz will never agree to it, risking equipment and troops for the rescue of one man."

"I wasn't suggesting we went just for the Captain. Walker is held there too, and God knows how many others. If we can pull off a rescue mission, it will not only bring back troops, but it could provide a massive morale boost to everyone here."

"I am not sure the General will see it that way."

"Then to hell with him. We'll do it on our own!"

"It's worth us at least putting it past him before we go it alone. If we do this without authorisation, there will be hell to pay even if it is a total success."

"Whatever the price, it's worth paying over letting our people be at their mercy."

Chandra smiled.

"You know, I remember a time when Jones told me that you were a man to never break the rules. A marine who obeyed every command to the letter."

"We were not at war then. It gives a new perspective."

"And if you had heard about troops being taken captive, and they weren't friends of yours?" she asked.

"We'll never know. So what, if my personal friendship is affecting my judgement? We fight for each other, otherwise what is the point of it all?"

Chandra turned away and looked around the base at the hundreds of troops coming and going. She knew that General Schulz and Brigadier Dupont would likely not authorise it, but she had to ask.

* * *

The room was silent. The Major had outlined the information she had to the Generals, and they all sat awaiting Schulz's answer. He was in charge of all operations in the area, and they all looked to him. They didn't seem surprised that prisoners were being held, nor show much compassion for the soldiers' fate. They already knew and they do nothing, she thought. She panned around the room, looking for support from any of the officers, but they did their best to look away.

"No, I will not risk our people in a suicidal mission based on sketchy information. Your request is denied. I understand your desire to save your men, but this is not the time. You have done a fine job in this war, Major, and we need you to keep up the good work. With officers like you on the front line, we are bound to win the war. Your efforts will be greatly rewarded."

Fucking medals. My people are out there fighting and dying, for this? She was disgusted by the General's attitude, but she knew she was foolish for expecting anything else. He only cared about figures, not soldiers. She turned and strode out of the room without a salute. It was an insult to her superiors that she knew they could do little about. In a time when they needed every capable soldier they had, she could get away with a lot.

The Major stormed out of the Headquarters to find Taylor awaiting her. He could already see she had failed in her attempt to get the General's approval.

"Bastards," he muttered.

"I shouldn't have wasted my breath," she snapped.

"What now?"

"I won't leave our people there to rot. Find Phillips, he's the only one who can get us what we need."

"You think he'll help?"

"He's our only chance."

Chandra squinted as she peered over Taylor's shoulder. "There he is."

She brushed past Mitch to confront the Commander. He could already see that she wanting something from him and wasn't in the mood to accept anything less.

"What can I do for you, Major?"

"Glad you asked, we need to talk, now!"

She led the Commander back to their bunkhouse where she knew they would get some privacy. The Company was busy getting chow, and nobody would dare invade their space. Phillips was already restless by the time they reached the room, and he didn't like being led around. When they were finally shut inside the dorm room, the Commander opened his mouth to talk but was cut short my Chandra.

"The enemy are taking prisoners, and we think we know where. Captain Jones is almost certainly among them."

Phillips shook his head. It was clearly something he had heard before and had been the subject of much pressure from those around him.

"I have already heard this from the mouths of other officers who want to rush headlong into enemy territory to get them back."

"You knew and have done nothing?" shouted Taylor.

"What can I do? We have been losing ground since the day this war began, and we are lucky to ever hold on to anything for long. We have endless lists of dead, wounded and MIAs. General Schulz will not risk any more troops to pursue this. I am guessing you already know this, as you would only be coming to me if you had already failed with him."

"Damn straight!" snapped Taylor.

"What do you expect me to do?"

"I don't give a damn who's in charge of this base. Your

responsibility is to us. We have people out there left to the mercy of the enemy, and that includes at least two of your own. I expect you to do whatever you must to get them back!" shouted Taylor.

Phillips looked insulted and put out by Taylor's sudden lashing out.

"Must I remind you of the chain of command, Major?"

Chandra stepped forward. She could not take anymore.

"Don't give us that shit. We've been getting our arses blown off since this war began while you sat comfortably at command. We don't expect you to pick up a weapon and join us, but we do expect you to give us the support we deserve."

Phillips gasped as he lowered his head in shame. He knew it was wrong to leave troops behind, but he had treated the losses as pure statistics. He looked back up and spoke softly.

"If I help you, the General will have my balls."

"And if you don't, soldiers will die. We are going to find Jones, and any other prisoners, with or without your help. Without you, we go in blind and will likely pay a high price for it. With your assistance, we may just pull it off."

The Commander knew he was between a rock and hard place, but they had made a solid case. As much as he stuck to the rules, he despised both Schulz and Dupont.

"Alright, to hell with it. With the way things are going, there's probably little they can do to me anyway."

Taylor smiled as he patted the Commander on the shoulder.

"You're doing the right thing, Sir."

"I hope so."

"What intel do you have on this?" asked Chandra.

"We know prisoners are being kept in a facility in Metz in small numbers. What we don't know is why."

"What have we been doing since they arrived here?" asked Chandra.

Phillips looked up to the Major dumbfounded.

"We have studied them. We have tried to understand our enemy," mused Taylor.

Phillips nodded in agreement.

"You really think that's what they are doing? Studying our soldiers?"

"I'd be amazed if they weren't," replied Chandra. "Something tells me that this invasion has not resulted in the blitz success which they had hoped for. We are starting to slow their advance and adapt to better fight them. They may now be looking for every avenue to exploit."

"That would explain it. From what we can tell, they have only taken military personnel from the front lines."

"How many prisoners do you figure they have?"

"Maybe a dozen or more."

Taylor nodded. "Alright, few enough that we should be able to make this quick and quiet."

"Do you really believe you can get them out?" asked

Phillips.

"If we were able to take out the Poitiers weapon, we can do anything. With accurate information of their location, it is more than doable."

"Okay, I can get you maps and heat signature images from the area. I can authorise you on a mission to the west, but not for this purpose. Once you head for Metz, you will be on your own. You must be aware there will be repercussions for this even if you succeed."

Taylor nodded, but he didn't care what might become of them when they got back. He stared at the Commander until it became clear he had no desire to hear any more about it.

"I will help you get to Metz, but once you return, I cannot admit to any involvement. We cannot afford to have it know that command level officers have been subordinate in the face of such a conflict."

Taylor sighed. Typical fucking politician, he thought as he rubbed his brow. He looked over to Chandra to be certain he had her support. He knew she would take the brunt of the flack as the Company commander if she went along with it.

"You should let my marines do this alone, Major. You are needed with the Company. Better still, we're Americans, and there's only so much Schulz and that idiot Dupont can do to us."

It was clear that Chandra wanted more than anything

to go on the mission, but she held her tongue and thought a little longer.

"As much as it pains me to say it, you're right. I would never have you take this risk alone, but it may be the only way of keeping this Company together. With the reputation you have earned, you hold a lot of weight around here. A platoon of gung ho yanks going on a suicidal mission without orders is far easier to justify than the entire Company being implicit in the affair."

Taylor chuckled.

"For once our reputation may be what keeps us from the brig?"

"The Major is right. If you can pull this off, then the punishment will be minimal," Phillips added.

"Alright, that's it then. Taylor, you are now in command of the rescue mission which we will designate Operation Dead Stick. You will need to get Eddie Rains on board along with a second copter. He should be able to get another of the modified FVs if you ask nicely."

"I'm sure he'd be more than capable of the task and happy to help."

"Commander, I need all the intel you have on their location and enemy positions in and around Metz, and I need them before sundown. We are doing this tonight."

"Tonight? Don't you think that's a little hasty?"

"You're damn right it is," snapped Taylor.

"If command hadn't arsed around and waited on this,

we could probably have succeeded with a rescue attempt weeks ago and with far less risk. If we wait much longer, who knows where they will be or what situation the front line will be in."

"Major, are you sure it's worth all this risk? You could be throwing away your commission and many lives."

Chandra sighed. It was clear the Commander still did not understand the comradery that kept them together and made them one of the most effective fighting forces on the front.

"You just get us what we need, Sir, and let us worry about the rest."

Phillips nodded and stepped out of the room. He still didn't understand why they would rush headlong into such danger. It was a prime example of why they were both glad he was not on the front line with them.

"Phillips is a paper pusher and number cruncher," growled Taylor.

"Yep, and he's just the man we need right now. He has got to this level because he's suited to it. He'll come through for us."

She stopped and looked into Mitch's eyes. She was always fascinated by his utter lack of fear, or at least the appearance of it. Taylor had not hesitated to lead a rescue mission for troops who were not even his countrymen.

"You sure you want this?"

Taylor nodded.

"And your marines?"

"Damn straight, they'd have volunteered just as quickly."

"The Commander is right. Even if this mission is a success, there will be hell to pay for it. We are directly contradicting General Schulz's orders. On top of that, the aliens aren't going to be too impressed with us snatching up their prisoners from under their noses. There could be major retaliation, and that retaliation will be blamed on us."

Taylor shook his head in astonishment at how spineless their leaders were.

"I don't give a shit about Schulz. He's not the one out there fighting and dying for this planet. Those creatures are coming for us whatever we do, so this will only reinforce the fact that we are still well in the fight."

Chandra nodded with agreement. She was finally convinced beyond all doubt that it was the right move. She knew her close friendship with Jones could cloud her judgement, and it would be the first target of any inquiry. She didn't care any longer. British forces were amassing for an action, and the worst that Schulz could do would be to send her back home; where her own forces would be more than happy to gain such a combat-experienced officer.

"This is your mission, but if there is anything I can do, you only have to ask," stated Chandra.

"I need the Reitech suits and gear. Beyond that, it's

best you stay out of it. Continue on with your posting to base security and rest up. I'm heading to find Rains and convince his crazy ass to give us a lift."

"Alright, we'll be at the western perimeter defences from 1800 hours on. You can collect the gear from there."

* * *

"What do you want, Major?" asked Eddie.

Taylor smiled as he watched the pilot make adjustments with a long bar spanner beneath the fuselage of his prized custom Eagle.

"Why would you think I'd be after anything?"

Eddie looked at the Major with a suspicious and knowing grin.

"Because you don't hang out at an airfield. You're only ever here when you have a mission or those few times after too many drinks."

Taylor coughed. He'd hoped Eddie had forgotten those drunken escapades.

"It's alright, Major. I'll be the last one to shop you. So what can I do for you?"

"You are aware that Captain Jones is MIA?"

"Yeah, I heard that, damn shame."

"Well, we believe that he is alive, along with Private Walker who was with him, and a few other missing troops."

"They find refuge somewhere?"

Taylor shook his head with a serious and taut face that made Eddie curious.

"Not exactly."

The Lieutenant put down the tool and got up onto his feet. He stared into Taylor's eyes as he tried to make some sense of the situation and the Major's intentions.

"Give it to me straight, Mitch. I'm a busy man these days."

"The enemy are taking prisoners. We don't exactly know why, but we have good intel they are alive and where they are being held."

Eddie shook his head as he smiled.

"Oh shit, you're not serious?"

"We have our orders."

"Bullshit! You'd only be coming here, personally, if you couldn't get this green lit by the brass."

Taylor smiled back. "You're a hard man to fool."

"So come on, you want me to fly you in and out on some crazy bitch mission to save POWs that you have been expressly forbidden from doing?"

"That about sums it up, yeah."

Rains turned and sighed as he paced up and down for a moment.

"Well, hell yeah, I'm your man. We're needed more than ever, not like they can fire us."

He thrust out his greasy hand to shake, which Taylor gladly accepted.

"Just one other thing, we're going to need two of these birds."

"Not a problem. General White has sent over two of my squadron to run equipment back and forth. When do you need us?"

"Tonight."

"I'll have to fix some paperwork, but we're in."

"Just to be certain, you realise the kind of shit you are entering into. We will have no chance of backup or recovery should something go wrong. Even if we succeed, General Schulz will want our balls."

"Hey, you gave me my orders, and I carried them out. How am I supposed to know who's in charge in this whole fucking mess?"

Taylor nodded in gratitude. "You're a good man, Eddie."

"Don't you forget it," he replied.

"Be ready for 2000 hours."

"We'll be here."

Taylor nodded and gave a grateful smile before quickly turning to go about his business. As he walked away, he shook his head in astonishment for what he, of all people, was about to undertake. He was gaining a reputation for disobeying his superiors, but the troops continued to love him for it. I'm doing it for all us, he thought to himself. He knew it was more personal than that, but it was at least some justification for his actions.

The Major paced back from the landing zone through the base with his head low in deep thought. Many troops from the different armies saluted or acknowledged him as he passed, but he didn't notice. Since the war had begun, he had been frequently left with few resources and allies. Now he walked among thousands of them, without any relief from the safety and comfort he had gained.

Jones must be alive, he thought. Despite their rivalry over the years, the two officers had become closer friends than he could ever have imagined. Captain Friday remained a loyal officer and good friend, but Jones was like a long lost brother to him. The death and destruction he had faced had, on occasion, brought him to utter despair; but not knowing Jones' fate was in some ways worse. As he approached the HQ bunker, he looked up to see Major Chandra stood blocking his path. She had a cheeky and confident smile on her face and stood with her hands on her hips.

"You get Eddie on board?"

"You get Phillips to cough up the data?"

"Damn right. Phillips can be a bastard, but when he knew we were willing to attempt a rescue of British soldiers, he was ready to do whatever I wanted. He'll never admit it officially, of course, unless he can take some of the glory without risking his standing."

"And that is why we are still lugging guns, and he's at a desk."

She nodded in agreement, and she quickly glanced around to be certain that nobody had heard their conversation.

"Eddie is good to go, 2000 hours."

"He's confident that he can get clearance?"

"Sure. Rains is a law unto himself, and since White has used him for special operations work, nobody is even sure who he reports to, beyond the General."

She stepped forward and leaned in a little closer.

"You sure you want to do this, now?"

He leaned back and stared into her eyes as if perplexed by the question.

"Is there really a choice?" he replied.

"Of course, there is always a choice."

"Leave no man behind," he mused in a slow and serious tone.

"Come on, Mitch, this isn't any kind of war this planet has ever seen. We've left scores of dead on our retreat across France. You can't tell me we haven't left soldiers to die."

Taylor shook his head.

"That doesn't make it right. Maybe we couldn't save the dead and dying. Maybe we couldn't recover the bodies of our comrades, but Jones is alive. I know he is."

She sighed as she thought about his words, and she wanted Jones back with all her heart.

"It's a dangerous path this one, you must know it. You

put Parker before all else, and you are doing it again for Jones."

"I am only human."

"No, we are soldiers, and we have a job to do. Our job is to fight, and if necessary, die in this war. We both want Jones back, just be certain you are doing it for the right reasons."

Taylor frowned as he turned and walked a few steps away from the Major. He knew she was right about his reckless breach of orders to save Parker. He turned and stepped back up to the woman he was growing to know as well as Jones.

"I may have blatantly disregarded our orders, but look where it got us. I saved a valuable Sergeant in my Company and have in turn, provided more than our fair share of service in these foreign lands. I have stood beside you, Major, as we both have Jones. He needs our help, and we need him back in this unit."

She thought about his words for just a few seconds before answering in a soft and friendly tone.

"Then I wish you every luck, and I only pray that if I am ever in trouble, I have you fighting my corner."

"You've got it."

He outstretched his hand and shook with Chandra.

* * *

Major Taylor stood and watched as his twenty-nine marines formed up before him. Every one of them wore the Reitech suits and related gear. Eddie was stood behind him in his usual ragged kit. He presented an anti-establishment image while being one of the finest officers Taylor had ever known. It was a fact that continued to amuse the Major.

"The General still not got you into regulation attire, I see?"

"No, Siree. He can tell me where and when to fly, and I'll follow it to the letter, but some things you just cannot accept."

"How on earth do you do it? I have never understood how you continue to get away with it."

"When you're the best damn pilot on the eastern seaboard, you get a little leeway."

He smiled as he stepped forward to address the troops. He was the only officer among them. He would not risk anymore of their command staff for what he knew was a reckless and dangerous mission. Sergeants Silva and Parker stood among them as the highest ranks.

Not one of them yet knew what the night had in store for them. He could see the questions they wanted to ask in their eyes. Formed up with the best hardware available and two modified copters, they all knew it was more than a regular patrol. They stood at attention as they eagerly awaited news of their duty.

The surrounding area was silent now. Only a few dimmed lights provided any view of the area. Rains' landing area had been kept isolated from the main base in order to give the crews priority for their main task. Their main duty was the transport of key components and personnel related to the Reitech technology. Nobody bothered them as few had the authority to do so. In the distance, they could see and hear vehicles and troops always on the move.

Gunfire continued to ring out every once in a while. The fighting died down at night, but it never fully stopped. Finally, the Major spoke to break the silence and feed the marines' appetite for information.

"Remember Amiens. Remember Captain Jones and Private Walker. Aside from myself, Sergeants Parker and Silva, you were all there. You witnessed the loss of our comrades, our brothers. New intelligence suggests they are alive, along with up to a dozen other POWs."

Gasps rang out across the two lines of troops.

"Sir, POWs?" asked Parker.

"I can speculate as to why they are keeping prisoners, but that's all it would be. All we know for sure is that prisoners have been taken in small numbers, and that Jones and Walker are likely to be among them."

"How have you found them, Sir?"

"Heat signatures. The enemy body temperature is either far lower than a human, or their armoured suits hide it."

"So where we heading, Sir?" asked Silva.

"To the city of Metz."

Several of the marines gasped. A few weeks ago it would have meant little to them. They neither knew where it was nor cared. But now they knew the terrain and the enemy's location, and it was a grim fact to swallow.

"Sir, that's way beyond the enemy's front line, and we know Saarbrucken is crawling with the bastards."

"That's why we've got Eddie here. Lieutenant Rains, along with Lieutenant Kato, will be flying us in. I know this is a lot to ask," he stopped and sighed. "We pulled off Poitiers, so you can't tell me we can't make this work."

"What kind of trouble we expecting?" asked Sugar.

The burly gunner stood confidently. Taylor looked down at the vast weapon in his arms and smiled. He carried one of Reiter's newly designed weapons, but he had bolted it together with his old light machine gun. The bastardised weapon looked so large that it should be vehicular mounted. Yet Sugar stood casually with it resting across his arms. He watched the Major stare at the weapon that he held like his own baby.

"I won't lie to you. I have officially requested permission for this rescue mission and been denied flat out by General Schulz. I cannot order any of you to follow me here, but I am unwilling to leave our people at the mercy of the invaders."

He turned and paced down the line before the marines. None of them spoke as they all took in what Taylor had said. They knew that disobeying direct orders from the General was not a situation to be taken lightly. Mitch took a deep breath to calm him before continuing.

"The General has not fought among us. He has not watched his friends be killed every day of this war. He has not stood firm against all odds and fought to the bitter end. He may yet be a good leader, but he is not one of us. We are numbers on a screen to him. He will not allow this rescue because he has made a calculated risk assessment of the resources that would be required for it. We are that resource."

He stopped and looked out across their faces that were shadowed in the low light.

"My friends are not a resource. We have made it this far by sticking together and fighting for each other. I refuse to give up on one another now. We have made it this far together. Anyone who wants no part in this may leave now without issue."

Taylor looked across the faces of the troops before him. He knew he couldn't rightfully force any of them to follow him in disobeying orders, but he prayed they would stand by him once more.

"Those who wish to sit this one out may fall out now and return to the Company!"

He stared into their eyes and each of them stared back. They all stood fast without a single flinch or doubt. The Major had won the respect and trust of everyone among them before the war had even begun. Now more than ever, they would follow him to hell and back.

"I am not bullshitting you here. There could be hell to pay for this even if we succeed. But for me, there is no punishment that our command could dish out that would not be worth paying for a chance to save our people."

"Sir, I think I speak for all of us. Let's do this," said Silva.

"Oorah!" Parker shouted.

The cry was repeated along the line and rang out across the open plain of the landing zone. Taylor smiled at the confidence they were placing in him.

"I cannot promise you anything from this mission, or the resistance we could face. I cannot say we will definitely get our boys out, but I can promise you we will do everything in our power."

"You point the way, Major, and we'll do the talking," said Sugar.

The hulking gunner grinned again as he stood still holding his treasured weapon.

"We're heading for Metz. All intelligence would suggest that the major mass of enemy forces are further east around Saarbrucken, but that doesn't mean we'll have an easy run of it. The copters should be able to get us in without resistance if we fly low through the valleys and stay out of trouble."

"Sir, do we have an extraction plan?" asked Parker.

BATTLE EARTH III

"We've got Rains and Kato here who will stick with us where possible, but aside from them, no. Nobody but those here and Major Chandra know of our intentions. The most assistance she could provide us with is her pleading with the Generals to help. They have already shown they will not risk assistance to save those prisoners, so I would not expect them to extend any more help for us."

"Shit, a suicidal mission behind enemy lines. Sounds just like our kind of gig," roared Silva.

Chuckles rang out across the lines. Taylor appreciated them making light of the situation. It was the only way to stay sane.

"Parker and Silva will lead their own sections, and the rest of you are with me. Remember what it's like to fight on their terms. No radio links means we need to stay close. This new gear we have got has made it a fair fight, but let's keep the odds in our favour. Sections stay in visual contact at all times. Any questions?"

The landing zone remained silent.

"Alright, load up, and let's get our people back!"

The troops separated and began shuffling quietly into the copters. A sombre tone fell over the landing zone as they all considered the danger they were facing. Going deep into enemy territory, and without hope of backup or assistance, was a daunting task. They had only done it once before to destroy the enemy weapon in Poitiers.

Destruction of the invaders' super weapon had been

seen as the only hope for humanity's survival. They had accepted it might have been a suicide mission and gotten on with it. Now their lives seemed to carry more value, but they knew they had a responsibility to the prisoners to bring them back. Taylor noticed light footsteps approaching and turned to see Major Chandra step out from the darkness.

"You said you'd stay out of this."

She nodded.

"And I will, but I could not let you set off alone. It's a grim day that our own people are giving up on each other. Perhaps this can go some way to reinforcing the value of our soldiers' lives. Men and women from every nation have given everything they had to give."

"You may support us in spirit, Major, but it is vital that you isolate yourself from this mission. You could lose command over the Company should your involvement be known."

Chandra sighed. She was stuck in an abominable position.

"I hate this. I must turn my back on comrades to save others."

"You're doing the right thing. The Company has tight bonds, and we cannot lose that. General Schulz would gladly split the unit."

"I'd like to see him try. He may be in charge of this front, but he is not a British officer. We have more than earned our right to stand together as one."

Taylor nodded in agreement. For years he had trained against the British in friendly exercises, and they had been their best competition. Never could he have imagined to have become one with them. He looked down at the slight Indian officer and smiled at her. Her stature hid her strength of character and body well. Now before him in the Reitech suit, she was dwarfed even further.

It made him think of his brutal mauling at the hands of Karadag, the alien Commander. The memory ignited a spark of pain to soar through this body. His wounds had largely healed, but the aches and pains were far from gone. He did his utmost to hide it from his comrades, and they respected him further for soldiering on.

"Have you got anywhere on securing Reiter the resources he needs?" asked Taylor.

"Barely had a chance since we got onto planning this mission."

"Last time I came up against one of those alien bastards in close quarter, I got my ass kicked. Every time they get close, we get torn apart. I never thought I would see the day when we would need to fight hand-to-hand, but it doesn't change the fact that it has been thrust upon us."

"I hear you."

"That shield technology could work if Reiter can just get it to an operational level. I know he has some ideas on a close quarter weapon, so push him."

"You think he'll still be working at this time?"

"Trust me, that man doesn't sleep. He only works."

"Then I'll get on it and good luck tonight."

"Thanks, we'll see you at dawn."

He turned and paced up the ramp of the copter to see that his marines were sat along the fuselage in readiness. He turned to Rains who was awaiting his signal. He gave a nod. It was all the Lieutenant needed. The engines powered up, and they knew there was no going back.

CHAPTER THREE

The copters soared through a thickly wooded valley towards their target. Taylor watched the shadows of the imposing trees flash by just twenty metres from the windows. Having sat down with nothing more to do but ponder his actions, he was starting to realise how much trouble he was stirring up. He had broken orders to save Parker, but that was in the heat of a battle. This time it was different, and he knew it.

"I guess Schulz will have your balls for this?" asked Silva.

He looked up at the calm and confident Sergeant. Their two sections rode with Rains. Sergeant Parker and her team were with Kato.

"Schulz can tough talk as much as he likes, but he needs us," growled Taylor.

"You think that'll be enough to save us from the can?"

Taylor shrugged his shoulders. He wanted to believe that it was true, but he also knew that his insubordination could not go unchecked. Never before had he simply deemed his orders to be unjust and unreasonable. Perhaps Schulz will see he was wrong if we pull this off, he thought. He shook his head in response to his own question. Schulz was a bastard and wouldn't ever change.

He looked down the line of marines and admired their resoluteness. They were just as calm and cool headed as if on a training exercise. He wondered how much was down to their training and discipline, and how much to do with the death and destruction. After all they had witnessed, he wondered if they had become accustomed to the thought of death and the loss of friends.

The Major had never asked his marines whether they should even be risking themselves for two British soldiers. The two units had become so integrated that they rarely saw a distinction anymore, unless it was for the sake of a quick joke. He lifted up his Mappad and studied the surveillance images one last time.

Heat signatures showed that up to a dozen humans were being held in a prison just a few kilometres south of the city. It had been constructed a hundred years previously and was a vast sprawling complex which could house ten thousands criminals. He wondered what had become of the occupants after the area had fallen to the enemy. The guards had a duty to protect them and move them to safety. In reality, he knew that in the chaos of the invasion, many would have been left to their own devices.

Thinking about the prisoners for a few minutes, he wondered why there were not more signatures of the prison's inhabitants. He looked up to the Sergeant who he knew to be a smart and well-informed man.

"The prisoners, where do you think they are?"

Silva sighed as he looked away and back to Mitch.

"It was chaos getting everyone out of the cities. I guess they either let them loose or..."

His voice faded away as he thought about the alternative.

Neither man wanted to consider the slaughter that they both suspected. Most of the others weren't paying attention or didn't cotton on to their train of thought. Taylor nodded to the Sergeant. They both knew what they must prepare themselves for. Taylor sat back against the fuselage and relaxed as much as he could for the last few minutes of peace they would have.

There was barely anymore than a little light from the moon piercing into the cabin of the craft. Their vision had adjusted to the darkness. Night vision equipment was on general issue to most of their forces before the war, but the enemy's energy weapons made them dangerous to use. A pulse from their energy blasters would blind and temporarily incapacitate anyone wearing them. Taylor now only used the night vision in his binoculars to survey scenes.

Lacking visibility in night combat was a scary situation to be in. Taylor would avoid night combat at any cost with the alien invaders. But with so much ground to cover in enemy territory, they were left with little choice.

Eddie cut the power to the copter's engines, leaving only the retrofitted alien technology to provide propulsion. They hoped it would cover their approach as it had done before. It was clear the invaders had not yet learnt their lesson. They were clearly still ignorant of the threat the humans could present.

Taylor looked at the Mappad at their position as they came down slowly on a small access road, half a kilometre from the prison's eastern perimeter. In an ideal world, they would put down right over the POWs' position, but they had little of idea what to expect. The ramps thumped down into the soft and muddy ground that squelched as the heavily laden marines hit the ground. Parker rushed down her ramp, but left her section aboard.

"Sergeant, you will wait here and be ready on our signal. The flares could attract a lot of attention, so we'll only use them if we have to and keep them to a minimum. Can you remember the colour identification?"

"Yes, Sir."

He turned and nodded to signal for Silva and the others to follow him towards the perimeter wall. They had landed between thick trees in a well-hidden position. The two sections continued on quietly in their columns with Taylor at the head. He had clipped his Mappad device onto his left arm, allowing him to keep his rifle at the ready. The threat and surrounding danger was beginning to set in. They were all alone in occupied lands.

You'd better be alive, Jones, he thought. Without the rescue of Jones and the others, he would be in more trouble with his superiors than he could imagine. Could it be any worse than death? He thought about it a little more as he paced on in darkness. He knew that the one thing Schulz could do was remove him from his Company. After all their struggles to fight and survive, he could not bear the thought of being parted from them. Would that be the price of saving soldiers? To then be parted from them?

Taylor reached the end of the road and a small verge that overlooked the prison. He lifted his hand and signalled for them to halt. Silva moved up beside him to survey the situation. The main facility lights were on. They could see the city lights of Metz glimmering to the north. The unmanned nuclear power plants had kept power to the areas where cables were not obliterated by the war.

The outer fences of the prison still lay in darkness. Taylor pulled out his night vision binoculars and panned across the perimeter that was less than a hundred metres ahead of them. He nodded as he quickly identified four drones waiting silently in front of the easterly gate. The entrance was small and lightly guarded.

"Must be a secondary entrance," he whispered.

Silva lifted his night vision goggles and held them before his eyes. The body of the device knocked into the brim of his helmet, and he cursed at the clumsiness of how they had to use the equipment. Taylor smiled at his discomfort, but the Sergeant merely continued to survey the scene.

"Going to make a whole lot of noise taking 'em out," he replied.

"Do we have another choice?"

"We could circle the perimeter and look for a quieter way in."

Taylor shook his head. They were walking into the unknown and in hostile territory. Had there not been friendlies within the compound, he would avoid it at all costs.

"Once we start firing, all hell's gonna break loose anyway. I say we take out these drones now and be rid of them."

Silva nodded. It was as good a plan as any.

"Spread out. Advance fifty metres, open fire on my signal, and fire up an F4 flare as soon as the guns start firing."

"You want them going in before we're even through the gate?" asked Silva.

"The second the guns start firing, we are working against the clock. We don't have a choice."

Silva nodded. Taylor moved forward over the verge, and the Sergeant stood in position, relaying the commands to the troops as they followed after the Major. The Reitech suits allowed the marines to move effortlessly with the weight they carried. The only sound was that of their boots squelching in the open field.

Taylor could feel his heart rate increase with each step as they quietly closed the distance. They still had little idea of the drones' capabilities in terms of identification. A vast noise bellowed in the sky, causing all the troops to quickly drop onto one knee and duck to conceal themselves the best they could. They've found us, thought Taylor.

He waited for a moment to see what was approaching. The booming grew louder until the ground vibrated beneath them. They could do nothing but remain still, and wait and hope they had not been spotted. A slab fronted and bulbous ship rushed overhead and slowed as it entered the prison complex airspace.

Taylor gasped in relief that it appeared to be unrelated. He looked around at the faces of the nearest marines to see the same glimmer of satisfaction. He turned back to track the vessel. Beam lights burst into action as it came in to land in one of the courtyards. The entire underbelly was lit up as well as the ground below it.

The Major turned the bevel on his binoculars to return to normal magnified vision and lifted them to his eyes. He could see the vehicle come in to land, but it was largely obscured by one of the vast detention centres between the vessel and their position. He squinted to make out a glimmer of movement a few moments later.

Finally, through a small gap between two of the buildings, he could make out the sight of humans being led from the vessel. A Mech strode past in between them with its huge cannon slung casually across its armoured forearms. Shit, they must be bringing more prisoners in. We better have enough space to get them out.

The marine platoon waited and huddled in the grass for twenty minutes. They knew the drones were close but had not identified them. Their mission presented enough danger without having to take on the guards of the transport vessel. Taylor did not have to relay commands. They all knew they must wait.

The vessel finally began to lift off from the base and head quickly off to the east. Taylor waited until it was well clear, and he could no longer hear the intimidating boom of its engines. He knew they had a narrow margin to make the mission work. When he was absolutely happy that they were left in peace once again, he turned to the troops and gave them the nod to move forward.

Taylor lifted himself to his feet. His knees creaked from sitting like a statue for what felt like an hour. He stretched his muscles and flexed his joints until he softened up and then moved forward at a slow and quiet pace. Taylor lifted his rifle and quickly targeted the first Mech. The moonlight glimmered off its metallic structure.

He looked back at his marines, but they had already stopped and readied themselves to fire upon seeing his weapon raised. The time for covert action was over. He nodded to Silva for the Sergeant to ready the flare. The Major turned back to his target and took in a deep breath. He pulled the trigger and fired three shots off in rapid succession. The drone was smashed over onto its side as gaping holes were torn in its body.

The moonlit field pulsed with light as the platoon opened fire with a rapid and brutal volley into their targets. The drones were all destroyed before they could return a single shot. The signal flare burst above them and lit up the scene. Taylor quickly leapt to his feet and rushed forward, shouting for his marines to follow him. They reached the gates of the prison and the burning wrecks of the drones. Their new weapons had left the alien devices as heaps of scrap.

Taylor's gun fired once again as he rushed forward. The round hit the broad lock of the gates and blew a hole through it and the surrounding mesh. The platoon rushed through without stopping and continued at a quick pace along the smooth concrete ground. Two Mechs quickly appeared from between two buildings up ahead but were utterly overwhelmed.

Fire poured from the marines as they continued rushing on. Each Mech was hit with half a dozen shots.

Their bodies had barely hit the ground by the time marine boots were thundering past. Taylor came to a quick stop to identify his surroundings. He had only seen the layout of the facility from aerial surveillance.

Silva's section rushed to his side and took up positions behind a narrow wall, as the Major surveyed their location. Doors burst open to their left flank and three Mechs rushed out to fight them in a futile attempt. Fire ripped into the guards, and Taylor nodded with satisfaction at the realisation that their equipment was finally up to the task. Although he knew a surprise attack in numbers was a long way from a pitched battle.

Kato's copter flew overhead before Taylor could get to his feet. The craft's nose lifted quickly, and the tail dipped to swoop in for a fast descent. They came to a hover just twenty metres above the building where they had identified the heat signatures of humans.

"That's our target," called Taylor.

He quickly looked around at the dozens of other detention rooms just like it on the facility.

"Sergeant Silva, check out these other buildings and secure the area!"

He leapt to his feet and ran towards the target building. He didn't have to give the order to his section. They were already close behind. Taylor could see out of the corner of his eye that Parker's section was already dropping onto the roof above. Their boosters provided for a soft landing despite their heavy gear that went unheard over the sound of the engines.

Taylor was first through the door as he threw caution to the wind. His desire to save his friend had affected his judgement, but he only realised it too late. As he burst into the entrance, he was met by the sight of a gun barrel just a few metres away. The Mech holding the weapon fired before he could raise his rifle.

The corridor flashed with light as the pulse smashed into the Major's torso. The power of the blast launched him onto his face and tossed him to the ground like a ragdoll. The Major was conscious for just long enough to feel the pain of the impact as he slid along the corridor and smashed into a sidewall.

Sugar stomped into the corridor and stood his ground before the body of his Major. He opened fire with both of his weapons on full auto. The Mech got off two shots as he rained down fire that smashed the creature back, causing its weapon to miss the hulking marine by just a metre. He bellowed with all the air in his chest as he emptied both magazines into the creature and a second that tried to come to its aid.

The corridor lit up with flames as the walls caught fire under the heat and concentration of the rounds. The two creatures were reduced to twisted piles of scrap. Sugar's weapon clicked empty, and he lowered his weapon to quickly check on Taylor. He looked back up for just a moment to see that he was safe and then leapt to the Major's aid.

"Major!" he shouted in hope of a response.

He grabbed hold of Mitch's shoulders and shook him. The rest of the section ran into the entrance of the building to see the horror of their leader lying lifeless. Sugar knelt down and listened to his breathing.

"He's alive!" he barked.

The marine got back up and looked at the smoking armour that lay across Taylor's chest. The round had gouged over a centimetre out of the armour but had not penetrated. Sugar shook him again in desperation. An explosion rang out further into the building, and Sugar glanced down the corridor. Gunfire followed it, and he quickly reached to change his magazines. Two of his section ripped fire extinguishers from the wall and rushed to the flames.

The towering Sugar jumped as he felt a hand grasp his wrist. The shock almost made him reach for the trigger of his weapon, but he looked down to see the Major grasp his arm with a surprisingly firm hold. His eyes were open wide, and he had a stunned expression as he stared blankly at the marine. Sugar's heart almost stopped as he realised Taylor was still alive. A smile broadened across the man's face.

"You gonna help me up, or keep looking like you wanna kiss me?" Taylor jested.

Sugar took a hold of the Major's arm and hauled him to his feet. Mitch groaned as pain soared through his body. He'd almost gotten used to not feeling like a total wreck.

"You okay, Sir?"

Taylor nodded. He lifted up his rifle and turned at the sound of gunfire. He suddenly realised where he was and their purpose for being there. He shook his head to try and wake himself up and then looked to Sugar and the others who were awaiting his orders.

"Let's get our people back. Let's go!"

They all cheered as they rushed forward to the end of the corridor. Campbell led from the front; his beloved sniper rifle slung on his back and a Reitech rifle in hand. Taylor winced as he hobbled forward. His neck creaked in agony, and his arm was numb. His spine was only saved from breaking on impact with the wall by the rigidity of his armour. It was little consolation when it hurt so much.

Gunfire erupted in the corridor ahead before the Major could get around the corner. He heard a cry of pain as Allen, one of his section, was struck in the arm. The Private collapsed back against the wall as the others kept firing. Energy pulses rushed down the corridor and blew gaping holes in the space between the wounded man and Taylor.

"Fuck!" bellowed Allen.

The Private screamed at the top of his voice. Taylor could see that the shot had dislocated Allen's shoulder and taken the flesh down to the bone. He turned to see Campbell huddled behind a metal-wheeled cart that had already taken a blast from the enemy. He peeked around the corner just enough to catch a glimpse of the enemy as a burning pulse of energy zipped past his head and narrowly missed singeing his eyebrows.

The section took cover in doorways and behind trolleys like Campbell. They could barely get a shot off under the hail of energy blasts. Taylor could make out a single fallen Mech further along the corridor, but they had done little other damage. Corporal Hall looked back into the face of his leader.

"Sir, we need to get the fuck out of here!" he shouted.

Taylor looked back down at Allen who was still screaming in pain, and with no one attending to him. The Major was still stunned from the blast and had frozen. He looked back into Hall's eyes with an expression that put the fear of God into the Corporal. Hall leapt across the hallway between enemy fire and reached the adjoining corridor from where the Major had been watching.

He grabbed hold of Mitch by his arms and threw him back against the wall. Hall had only been Corporal for a week, and promoted not through experience or natural progress. He was filling the shoes of a dead marine. Taylor hit the wall hard, and his armour clunked hard against the thick wall that jolted him. He looked at the Corporal in utter shock.

Taylor still looked dazed and did nothing to push him back whilst gunfire continued to rain down the corridor beside them. Hall slapped the Major hard across the face. The Reitech suit made the strike land harder than he had planned, and Taylor's head snapped quickly around. He immediately turned back with blood dripping out of his mouth. His eyes squinted, and Hall could see life return to his leader.

Mitch took a firm grasp on Hall and wrestled him quickly back against the far wall, and with his left arm depressed into the Corporal's throat so that he couldn't breathe. As the man choked, he looked around to see further light pulses smash into the wall just a metre away and blast through it. Dust sprayed out into the air all around them. He looked back to the Corporal who was starting to lose colour in his face. He quickly released his grip, and Hall did his best to stand tall.

"That's more like it," he croaked.

Taylor looked down and saw two grenades slung on the marine's webbing. He let go of his rifle and let it rest on its sling. He pulled out the grenades and twisted the firing cap of the first.

"Sir, the prisoners!"

Taylor remembered his order to not use any explosives during the raid as they could endanger the POWs. He thought for just a second before leaping to the edge of the corridor and tossing one with all his strength. The exoskeleton suit caused the grenade to be blasted down the corridor as if he had hit a home run. He twisted the cap of the other and quickly launched it after the first. He turned back and looked at the surprised Corporal who had just gotten his breath back.

"We aren't rescuing anyone if we stay pinned here!" barked Taylor.

An explosion rang out along the corridor and was quickly followed by a second. The armoured leg of a Mech fired down the corridor and struck the wall. Campbell was bounced along the ground to the Major. Two of the marines got up for a better look but could barely make anything out through the dust cloud created by the blast.

Just as the marines were readying themselves to fire once again, a burst of fire rang out from down the corridor.

"Those aren't Mech guns!" shouted Campbell.

"Keep down!" bellowed Taylor.

They remained huddled behind what was left of their cover as a volley of fire rang out beyond the dust cloud. Taylor coughed as the thick dust lined his lungs. Parker, you came for us, he thought. Just as he had broken orders to save her, she was doing so for him. It was not something he liked to encourage, but he liked living as much as the rest of them.

Silence suddenly fell upon them. Their ears were still ringing from the constant fire and explosions. The interior of a room beside them smoked and flickered with flames. Then they could make out the sound of footsteps stomping across the debris of the surrounding rooms. Sergeant Parker appeared through the smoke at the head of her section.

She stood with her hand on her hip, and her rifle slung on her shoulder, looking down at the marines huddled in the ruined corridor. Allen groaned again, and the others finally jumped to his aid. Taylor knelt down beside the man as Campbell checked the wound. The Private was doing all that he could to hide the pain. Tears seeped from his eyes, but he stayed strong.

"How bad is it, Sir?" he asked.

"You'll be back in action in no time," insisted Taylor.

Allen nodded in appreciation, but he was sceptical. He looked down at the wound as Campbell lay a dressing over it. He winced as he looked at the damage. He couldn't move his arm and knew it would be a long time before it fully recovered, if ever.

"Am I going to sit out the rest of the war?"

Taylor shook his head. He knew it was a distinct possibility, but he didn't want the man to lose heart.

"Count yourself lucky, you just earned yourself a few weeks with a soft bed and to be waited on by a few cute nurses."

Allen smiled as he gritted his teeth.

"I need you to walk, Private. Can you do that? We cannot afford to leave people behind now."

He nodded in agreement as Campbell helped him up from his good arm. Taylor was satisfied that they could move. He turned to look at Hall and stared into his eyes. He was saying thank you without making it public. The Corporal smiled back in acknowledgement. A year ago Taylor would have had the marine on a charge for what he had done, but now he knew not everything was black and white. He turned to Parker.

"Any idea where the prisoners are?"

"Just a few corridors west, according to our maps. We were en route when we heard you were in trouble."

"Much resistance on the roof?"

"No, Sir. We entered the building without contest and only encountered four hostiles before we found you."

"Alright, any casualties?"

Parker shook her head.

"Good. They were arrogant not putting the proper defensive measures into effect here. If they think anything like humans, it'll drive them nuts that we've pulled this off under their noses once again."

Laughs rang out from a few of the marines as he lifted his rifle in readiness.

"Parker, you lead the way. Let's get our people back."

She turned and quickly went about her orders. The dust had largely settled, and as they continued on down the corridor, they could see the results of their work. The bodies of at least eight Mechs were scattered across the ground and through doorways that had been blasted from their hinges. The creatures' now familiar blue blood seeped out from dismembered sections of their armoured suits.

Hall spat on the body of the most intact alien as he strode past. Nobody thought anything of it. This was not a human enemy to feel sympathy towards. They hated the Krycenaeans with all the fibre of their beings. Yet they didn't even know their real name yet or understand their purpose for being on Earth.

A few minutes later, Parker stopped the column of marines to listen. As their heavy boots came to a stop, they could all hear the sound that had caused her reaction. Screams for help rang out through the corridors. They were muffled through the thick walls but were not far away.

"It's them!" cried Campbell.

Taylor strode up to the front of the column to stand by the Sergeant. Her eyes always appeared to shine brighter upon seeing him. It was obvious to all but a fool that they were in love, even though they rarely admitted it to themselves. The thought of losing each other was something both tried to ignore as much as possible. It was impossible to think of a world where they did not serve beside each other and share a bed afterwards.

The Major turned back to look at the marines who eagerly awaited their orders. Many were smiling at the prospect of finding fellow soldiers alive. He lifted up his Mappad and once more surveyed the images.

"I want this done smart and right. We have a fork up ahead. Parker's section head right, and we'll go left. Go room by room, and be aware of your surroundings. Keep your guard up. Let's move."

Taylor turned and quickly rushed forward before Parker could take a step. He wanted to do it right, but he also wanted to be there first. He reached the fork in the corridor and instinctively huddled in against the edge of the wall, creeping around for a better view. He half expected to find enemies awaiting him, but the corridor was empty. He waved his section on and rushed down the corridor. He couldn't believe he was within seconds of finding his missing comrades.

He had come so close to giving up hope that he kicked himself forever doubting their survival. Then his stomach turned at the realisation that he still had no idea if it was Jones and Walker imprisoned in the facility or some other poor devils.

"Help!"

The cries grew louder as Taylor rushed as quickly as he could while being cautious. He reached a locked cell door and saw a human face on the other side. A soldier with a scarred face and dry blood congealed on his skin. His voice was still muffled by the thick glass window, but Mitch could make out the strong French accent. Two other soldiers were huddled either side of him trying to get a peak, but he couldn't get a view of their faces.

"Back up! Away from the door!" shouted Taylor.

He pointed for them to move back and the command was quickly understood. He lifted his rifle as the rest of his section formed up around him. They guarded each side of the corridor, but most were fixated on the door to see who was held within. The dim area lit up as the Major's rifle fired into the lock, blasting a hole into the thick metal. A second shot quickly followed to finish off the high security mechanism.

There was just enough room to get a grasp on the rim of the door. Mitch reached in and pulled hard. The heavy door was flung open and crashed against the wall. Two men and a woman appeared, desperately trying to get out. He pushed forward to get into the cell. On a bench was Captain Jones with Walker lying in his arms.

The Captain looked up with a pale face. He looked like a man who had been utterly defeated. Only a glimmer of hope flashed in his eyes as he recognised the man who stood before him. Charlie studied Taylor for a minute, shocked at how different he looked. The Reitech armour and weapons were nothing like anything he had seen before. To him it resembled their enemy more than their own forces.

Taylor's face was as bloody and scarred as his own. The Captain looked weak and malnourished, and he had obviously lost a number of kilos in bodyweight during his imprisonment.

"Is it really you?" he asked.

Charlie looked suspicious, as if it was all too good to be true.

Taylor paced up to the two men and looked down at Walker. The man was taking his last few breaths. Dried blood stained his uniform from an old wound in the shoulder. Mitch looked up to Jones for an answer to the soldier's condition. Jones merely shook his head, signalling that Walker was a goner.

"Sir, we've got to get the fuck out of here," said Hall.

He was stood in the doorway impatiently. Taylor turned and held up his hand to stop the man.

The Major knelt down beside the dying soldier who was gasping to say a few last words. He outstretched his hand which Taylor wrapped his own around.

"Get me home."

"You can bet on it. We're getting you out of here."

"I want a proper burial, for my family..."

The man's voice faded, and his eyes began to contract as the life drained from him.

"A full ceremony, you'll have it all," replied Taylor.

Walker smiled faintly as he finally fell limp and passed over. Taylor looked up into the eyes of Jones who was still holding the dead soldier in his arms. Taylor looked down to see needle holes up the Captain's arms and continuing up and under his rolled up sleeves.

"Sir, we got to get our fucking asses out of here," whispered Hall.

Taylor turned and nodded in agreement. He looked back to the distraught Captain who he'd come to call one of his best friends.

"I have so many questions, but right now we haven't got time for it."

"I'm not leaving Walker behind," snapped Jones.

"I know," he replied. "Sugar, get in here!"

The huge marine ducked under the doorway and into the room.

"Can you carry Walker? We leave no man behind today."

Sugar reached down and carefully lifted the fallen soldier up and over his shoulder with little effort. He stood ready with one arm supporting Walker's body, and the other with his bastardised weapon held at the ready. Taylor knew the Reitech suits allowed them to do more than they could ever have imagined, but he wondered if Sugar would have done any different were he not wearing it. He turned back to Jones and the other three prisoners.

"Let's get you out of here."

He helped his friend to his feet and led him out the door. His excitement at saving his friend was largely numbed by the loss of their comrade, and the state he had found him. He wondered what they had been through, and if Jones would ever come back from it. At least he wants to live,

BATTLE EARTH III

thought Taylor. They reached the fork back the way they came and found Parker's section guarding the position.

"We're out of here, Sergeant. Fire the pickup flare as soon as we get outside."

Parker was fixated on the ruinous state of Jones and the fallen soldier being carried.

"Parker!"

She snapped out of it and looked into his eyes to see the sadness he was doing his utmost to hold back. She nodded and pulled the flare from her webbing.

"Alright, let's get the hell out of this shithole," growled Taylor.

He leapt forward to lead the two sections out. They'd heard nothing from Silva. He hoped that meant his section had met no resistance and set up a solid perimeter. They reached the corridor where they had entered the room, and he'd taken a blast in the chest, to find that parts of it were still burning and starting to spread.

Taylor burst out of the building to see Silva standing with a ghostly face in front of the opposing detention facility. The Major's heart stopped. What could be worse than what we have just found? he thought.

"Give me a sitrep, Sergeant."

Silva did not respond. He looked into the Major's eyes with the same lost expression that Mitch had seen in Jones.

"What's going on, Sergeant?" he insisted.

Silva turned and gestured for the Major to step through

into the building beside him. Taylor realised it was serious enough to warrant a look. He turned to the platoon.

"Take up positions. Parker! Get that flare up. Silva, you're with me."

The Sergeant begrudgingly agreed. It worried Taylor that one the toughest NCOs he had ever known appeared to be frightened to return into a building where he already knew what lay inside. Taylor looked to Silva's section, and they were as stunned as he was.

"Parker, you're in charge!"

He turned and gestured for Silva to lead the way. The demoralised Sergeant paced uneasily to the door and into the complex. As the door opened, the Major caught a blast of the revolting air that rushed from the building. He didn't ask what it was. The last thing he needed was to have the rest of the platoon as paralysed as the Sergeant.

Silva led him down a corridor until it opened up into a large hall that appeared to be designed for sports. Up ahead, he could see mounds of what looked like refuse. Can't be, he thought. Then it struck him, and his gut was right. Human bodies were piled high from the far wall to within ten metres of the corridor.

"My God!"

The two men stopped at the opening to the hall. Taylor gagged at the rotting stench that filled his nostrils and throat. Silva simply stood and gazed in shock. Taylor could see that most of the victims wore prison uniforms,

BATTLE EARTH III

although a number closer to them were soldiers.

"What were they doing here? If they only wanted to exterminate us, then why would Jones and the others be alive?" he asked.

Finally the Sergeant spoke.

"They are studying our soldiers, our warriors. These prisoners mean nothing to them. Looks like most of them were killed outright."

"What makes you think that?"

"Most of the prisoners have been slaughtered by gunfire. The soldiers have been experimented on. Needle marks all over, subjected to biological weapons."

"That's what they are doing here? Looking for our weaknesses? But why kill the inmates?"

"A few thousand criminals would have been a damn useful penal militia at the rate we are losing soldiers."

Taylor nodded and shook his head in disbelief simultaneously.

"I've seen enough," whispered Taylor.

The two men turned and strode back down the corridor with their shoulders slung low and their hearts heavy. They wanted it all to end.

"Incoming!"

The call echoed around the complex. Parker's voice was like a siren. Taylor felt his heart as he imagined the terrible fate they may have assigned themselves. Explosions erupted nearby that sent vibrations through the floor beneath their feet. Taylor and Silva snapped out of their depressive state as adrenaline soared through their bodies. They lifted their rifles, rushing to the doorway as the platoon opened fire.

As Taylor came to the opening of the building, he could hear the familiar and frightful sounds of the enemy jetpacks roaring as they came in to land. Ten metres from the door, he could see one of his marines lying lifeless on his side, but he couldn't make out who it was. Energy pulses smashed in all around them, but they were giving them hell in return.

The Major leaned out from the doorway to get an idea of their situation. He could see just four Mechs firing from the shelter of the next buildings. Another lay dead on the ground before them, it had clearly been knocked out of the sky on approach. Over the sound of the gunfire, he could just make out the sound of the engines of their copters approaching. He looked over to his section taking cover behind a thick wall.

"On me, now!"

Taylor rushed out of the building and took a sharp turn away from the enemy, and another turn to follow the perimeter of the building. He was sprinting at the limit the suit would allow. His turn of speed allowed them to reach the far edge of the structure quickly. Moments later they came up on the other side of the creatures with them in full view of their sights.

Taylor didn't wait and quickly targeted the first, hitting it with a burst of fire. Before the first creature had hit the ground, the rest of the section were into the open and firing. Within seconds, the prison went silent once again. Taylor didn't break stride to return to the platoon. He rushed up to the lifeless marine. Parker was stood beside the body turning it over.

"It's Sugar," she stated.

Taylor knelt over to check if there was any chance of him being alive. A pulse had struck his neck and burst through the windpipe, coming close to taking off his head. He had died instantly. Taylor shook his head in disbelief at losing yet another friend. Jones strode out from behind cover with the other POWs. They seemed unfazed by the incident, as if it was a part of their everyday lives.

Before Taylor could say a word, the two copters rushed into view and swept in low for a landing in an open hard standing just fifty metres away. It was at least some relief to see that their mission was over, and they could return to the lines that had become home. He righted himself and barked out his orders.

"Let's get moving! Go, go, go!"

He dragged the body of Sugar and headed towards Rains and Kato. Despite the assistance of the suit, the body sent striking pains through the Major's wounded body. He ignored the pain and said nothing. He would bare it for a fallen friend. As the copters hit the ground, their lights went out under blackout regulations. The two vehicles almost blended into the night of the unlit ground.

The marines rushed into the open doors of the vehicles to be greeted by the pilots from their seats. They were eager to get off the ground without even knowing of the perils that had been witnessed. Taylor passed Sugar's body onto another marine and waited at the door. Just as the last man stepped aboard, he heard a screaming engine blast across the skies. Leaning in through the door of the copter, he shouted to them all.

"Everyone silent, we've got incoming!"

They all knew what was being asked of them. They were hoping to go unnoticed and wait out their opponents. Seconds later, a small ship soared into sight and quickly landed down amongst the bodies of the creatures they had so recently despatched. Taylor pulled out his binoculars and zoomed in on the vessel as the door opened. Two Mechs strode out with their guns at the ready. Then Taylor gasped as a third figure appeared on the ramp, Karadag.

"Jesus Christ," he whispered.

He climbed carefully into the copter and crept up to Eddie's cockpit.

"Think you can outrun them?" he asked.

"Now they're on the ground, no problem at all. Button down the hatches and sit tight, Major."

Taylor nodded for the door to be shut and took his seat. He stared at Karadag through the window with his binoculars. The engines fired up, and the three creatures quickly turned their attention. Taylor's stomach was left on the floor as Eddie put down all the power he had. It was if their copter was lifted into the sky. They were safe and on the home run. But at what price? thought Taylor.

CHAPTER FOUR

The relatively short trip back over the battle lines was not the triumphant and celebratory experience Taylor had imagined and hoped for. Nobody said a word for the entire trip. Sugar's body was placed on the seats beside them. Allen laid back and tried to ignore the pain he was in. He was at least helped by a powerful dosage of painkillers. But Taylor could see that Jones' pain could not be numbed.

Taylor wanted to ask the Captain questions. So many questions he had rolled over in his mind. Now he didn't have the heart to ask them. His exhausted and beleaguered friend lay back in his seat next to Walker's body. Taylor no doubt realised that the two men must have forged a bond as strong as his and Charlie during their captivity, perhaps even more so.

Charlie Jones had been missing for just a matter of weeks, but he looked like a man who had spent years in the worst of conditions. His uniform was ripped and pierced. Taylor could make out slashes from bladed instruments and fresh scars beneath. He did nothing to hide the needle marks on his arms. The Captain was a proud man. He was a man who considered his image and steadfastness to be paramount in being a leader.

All of that was gone now. It had been replaced by a cold bitterness and a fear of what was awaiting him. He slouched back as if he was waiting for his own death and had come to accept it. Mitch wondered if he would ever get his friend back, or just a shell of a man who resembled him. When the copters finally touched down at the base they had left the previous evening, it was still in the pitch black of the night.

There was little relief at having returned to safety and having accomplished what they set out to do. When the door opened, and the ramp lowered, Taylor could make out a line of German military police. General Dupont was stood among them. It was a sight that made him sick. There was no welcoming party. No celebration of missing soldiers having been saved from a horrifying death.

The Major stepped out to face his fate with his shoulders slung low. He knew in his heart that he did the right thing, but the outcome was a long way from what he would consider ideal. Taylor knew from the moment they left the base, he would be placed on a charge even if the mission went exactly to plan.

Dupont rushed forward with his MPs as Taylor's boots hit the ground. He was disgusted by the fact they had no respect for the fallen and those that had been saved. They encircled the ramp as the marines disembarked. Rains climbed out to stop in shock at the sight.

"What is this shit?" he exclaimed.

"Major Taylor, you are hereby placed under arrest and to be transferred to the on base detention facility, pending an investigation and judgement by General Schulz."

"What the fuck!" shouted Rains.

He leapt from the copter and blocked the path between Taylor and the MPs.

"Just because Taylor, here, was the only one with the balls to get this done. You can't arrest an American officer, anyway!"

"Major Taylor was placed under the joint European command and will therefore comply with any ruling we make."

Rains tried to bellow out another argument, but Taylor interrupted him.

"Stop, Eddie."

The pilot turned in shock.

"You can't let this fly? This bullshit cannot stand!"

"I knew the price I would have to pay for this, and I have already accepted it."

"That's god damn bullshit!"

"We have a chain of command for a reason, Lieutenant.

To challenge it, is to bring discipline crumbling down around us. Whatever price I pay, it will be little compared to what they have been through."

He nodded in the direction of Jones and the other POWs. The weak Captain was hauling Walker's body off the copter with the last of his strength. Dupont's face changed to a look of utter shock as he stared at the gaunt figures.

"What the hell happened to them?" he asked.

He turned to Taylor for answers. The Major looked less than eager to explain. Dupont turned back to the MPs.

"Strip him of his weapons and armour, and take him away!"

He snapped back around and glared at the marines who looked on at him with a look of utter disgust and pointed at Silva.

"Sergeant, get these troops formed up!"

Parker stepped up to join them and wanted nothing more than to strike the General across the face. But she looked to Taylor and realised it was not the time. They had gotten themselves in more than enough trouble already. A medical crew rushed past the MPs to assist the rescued troops and take away the two dead and one wounded. Taylor watched as they were spirited away while he stripped off his equipment before his detainers.

The Reitech suit crashed to the ground as Taylor stepped from it and dropped his rifle. There was no more fight left in him. As he unclipped the last of his equipment, he turned to Silva who still ignored the General.

"Go about your duties, Sergeant. I'll be in touch soon enough."

The General hissed and sighed at the arrogance he perceived in Taylor. Mitch hated him with an even greater burning desire to strike him down. Silva turned and faced his men with a newfound confidence in defiance of the General.

"You heard the, Major. Form up!"

The MPs took up positions and led Taylor past the formed up platoon and away from the landing zone. Silva raised his arm in a salute that was quickly followed by the whole unit. Silva could feel the vehement hostility in the General without even looking at him. They had saluted a detained Major and not a General. Silva lowered his arm and turned his gaze to the General. He stared into his eyes as if asking for something from the man. The General sighed at the Sergeant's lack of respect for his position.

"Under the command of the Joint European Defence Force, you are hereby ordered to lay down your arms and equipment. You are to be confined to your billets until further notice. Rations will be brought to you when needed, and you will not leave those billets under any circumstances. Any man or woman found to be in breach of these conditions, will find them following in your Major's footsteps!"

The troops remained silent. Dupont knew that it was not out of respect for him. Finally, the Sergeant spoke up.

"Will that be all, Sir?"

Dupont coughed in surprise at the question. His face lit up in anger, but he knew there was nothing more he could do to the marines. Dupont nodded in agreement, turned and marched away to his vehicle, leaving the MPs to do their work.

"You heard the man. Lay down your weapons, and get some rest!"

It was an appealing thought but having to give up everything left a bitter taste among them. They could see trucks parked up nearby. Dupont was quite literally expecting them to remove their kit and hand it in, there and then. They began to strip off their weapons and armour and leave behind the exoskeleton suits which had done them such a good turn.

When Silva was done, he stood and waited for the last of them to lay down all that they had carried. One of the MPs stepped up to his side and spoke in a thick German accent.

"Your sidearm, Sergeant!"

Silva turned with an outraged expression.

"From my cold dead hands!" he snapped.

"You have your orders, Sergeant."

"This pistol was a private purchase, as allowed by my rank."

Silva spat on the floor beside the well-kept military policeman. He hated them in America as much as he did here, but at least his own people understood the law.

"This base is still US soil, is it not?" he asked.

The man nodded begrudgingly and could see the other marines becoming restless. He looked at the battle-hardened troops and sighed. Spineless bastard, thought Silva.

"Alright, NCOs may keep sidearms, but all other weapons, armour and associated issue equipment are to be removed!"

Silva smirked just a little. He enjoyed seeing how much it pained the MP to be told what's what. He turned back to the platoon and barked his orders.

"Fall out and return to billets!"

It further exasperated the MP that the Sergeant was not marching the platoon across the base, but he was at his wits end. Silva had enjoyed torturing the man but now thought back to their losses both on and off the battlefield. Parker strode up to walk beside him.

"What do you think they are doing with the Major?" she asked.

She could guess pretty well as much as Silva, but could not help but ask.

"He's in deep shit, no doubt. Schulz will want to make an example of him, and Dupont has lost face just as much. Nobody can doubt that the Major saved soldiers that should never have been left behind, but they will do everything they can do make him suffer."

She sighed.

"What else could he have done? Left our people there to die?"

"Schulz works on numbers. He's got dead and wounded back, and officers directly contravening his orders. As far as he is concerned, nothing good has come of this day."

"Fucking asshole! If only I could get my hands on him."

"You and me both."

"What will become of us?"she asked.

"Schulz will put us on some shit duties until he realises he needs us. We'll be alright."

"And Taylor?"

He looked into her eyes and could see her worry.

"If anyone can wriggle out from this, it's the Major."

* * *

Four weeks had passed, and the Major had seen nobody but his guards. The dim-witted and obnoxious military police revelled in their power over a high-ranking officer. The fact that he was American made them enjoy it all the more. He resigned himself to little more than exercising in his cell and lying in a dream for the rest of it.

Schulz can't leave me to rot forever. He hadn't received any news from his guards. He knew that he hadn't been moved, and so Ramstein had remained in human hands for all that time. It was some relief at least. But Taylor thought of his friends and his Company. What price were they paying for holding the line, and what crap had Schulz thrown them in to?

The more Taylor thought about his friends, the angrier he became that he was not able to be there for them. He tried his best to remain calm, but the sound of every vehicle and distant rumbling of artillery reminded him of them. Every night he was haunted by the hallowed eyes of Jones the last time he'd seen the Captain. He had long dreamt of getting his friend back, only to lose him again. They probably put him in a mad house, he thought.

Taylor's calm snapped, and he leapt up from his bed. He rushed up to the bars of his cage and whaled on them.

"Get me the fuck out of here! Get me out! Get me out!"

* * *

Chandra sat at the bottom of a muddy trench on the south side of the base. The occasional artillery round screamed overhead, but the line had become oddly tranquil over the last day. She sat with a mug of tea, treasuring the moment. She leaned back and looked up into the bright blue sky where there was not a cloud in sight.

Looking into the warm sky, she could forget for just

a few moments about the desolate landscape around her that had been ravaged by the war. Few trees stood that were not blackened and burnt. The roads had been smashed by artillery until the concrete and mud beside it mixed into almost uniformed rubble.

The defences of the base consisted of miles of trench works and bunkers. They were the only cover that would be erected in time. She could hear footsteps squelching towards her. The floorboards could only stave off the worst of the rain that rarely let up for more than a day or two. The footsteps were light. Gone were their Reitech suits.

They were reduced to the same frightened troopers that huddled underground and prayed to only tackle the enemy in vastly superior numbers. They were nothing compared to their enemy, man for man. Friday strode into view with a smile on his face. He rarely showed any dismay or sadness. Perhaps he hid it well, she thought.

"Major, we've just been sent a request for a platoon to fetch and carry."

She shook her head in disbelief.

"Will it ever stop?" she sighed.

"The General will get bored of punishing us eventually, I'm sure."

She turned and looked into his face to see if he really believed what he was saying. Friday always seemed so convincing that it was hard not to believe him.

"Relay the order and have a platoon get on it."

Friday turned to leave, but Chandra interrupted him.

"Captain, there's no rush..."

He turned around to see she was offering him a mug of tea. He smiled politely. Chandra could see he'd wished it was coffee, and that made her grin.

"All these years, and we still can't civilise you into the finer things."

He took the mug and sat down beside her. He sighed as his body creaked from being on his feet.

"Any news from the US?"

"Bits and pieces, but you probably know more than me."

"Na, my intel dried up a long time ago. You probably hear more around the mess than I get at briefings."

"Then there ain't a lot to say. Most of the major cities on the eastern seaboard are rumoured to have gone, and they're now dug in like us."

Chandra sipped back on her tea. They'd seen plenty of action the last few weeks, but nothing that came close to the seat of your pants fighting when Taylor was still around.

"You miss him, don't you?" asked Friday.

She smiled.

"Not in that way, Captain. Life was a whole lot more interesting with Taylor around. We were always at the forefront of the fighting, and we were making a difference every day. What are we now? Reduced to line duty. We're better than this, all of us, and wasted because a General got pissed off."

"Would you take it back? I mean, Taylor's mission. Would you have stopped him, having known what you do now?"

She shook her head.

"No, never! We had a responsibility to the comrades that had been lost. If the General couldn't see that, then that is his weakness, not ours."

"I hear it caused quite a stir among the Commanders, sounds like he didn't get off lightly either."

"That more scuttlebutt, Captain?" she asked.

Friday chuckled at her awkward usage of his services slang.

"No, Ma'am."

Chandra took some pleasure in the news. She'd heard as such herself, but it was nice to have it confirmed. Schulz should never have forced Taylor and herself into the situation. But with Commander Phillips gone, she had little influence or ways of changing their lot.

"Word is that the Reitech suits are out for issue, reckon we'll see 'em anytime soon?"

"Fat chance, Schulz will make it his mission to ensure that we never see such hardware again. He wouldn't want us to actually make any progress in this war?"

"Asshole."

She nodded in agreement.

"Our time will come again, Captain. We can't have come all this way to be relegated to the bench. The war is far from over, and we'll be needed soon enough."

A runner came hurtling down the trenches towards them. Monty appeared from around a corner and came to a quick halt in front of them.

"Ma'am, orders from command. They want a platoon to join a scouting party to the west."

"Why the urgency, Private?"

"Orders, Ma'am."

"Alright, relay them to Lieutenant Yorath, and have him follow out the orders."

Friday turned to the Major.

"It's alright, I'll do it. Yorath's been through enough shit. My platoon will handle it."

She nodded in gratitude for his kindness.

"Alright, Captain. You want it, you got it."

* * *

The heavy brig doors creaked along the corridor. Taylor knew the guards' routine. The only reason for their presence now would be to bring in a new prisoner, or escort one out. He didn't flinch from the position he lay in his bed. He'd been given nothing to read or to work his mind. Weeks passed with nothing to do but contemplate and replay recent events in his mind.

The sidewalls of the cell meant he could only see one other of the cages opposite him, but it was empty. He heard the wails of a few other prisoners held there, but they were mostly soldiers who had lost their minds. Four sets of footsteps approached. In his stay there, the Major had only ever heard two or three approach at any one time. He could already guess that their presence related to him.

As the steps got louder, the Major sat up in his tiny bed and rested back against the wall. He remained calm and slouched. He would never give those who detained him the satisfaction of feeling he was at their beck and call.

Two guards came into view and placed themselves either side of the barred door. General Dupont and his assistant strode up to the entrance and halted quickly at the bars. The Frenchman stared in at the Major with curiosity but made no request for the door to be opened. The four men stood before the bars of his cell as if waiting for his move.

"Can I do something for you gentlemen?" Taylor asked.

He knew that it infuriated the guards that he treated them like slaves. They rarely knew whether to treat him as an officer or a prisoner. They all knew that if he ever got out, and was cleared, he would make them suffer for any ill treatment.

"Major Taylor, you are well aware of the reason for your arrest and detainment," exclaimed Dupont.

"Yes, what of it?"

"I am here to inform you that you will face a military tribunal at some date in the future and that it may become plausible and realistic to do so at a time..."

"Get on with it, General."

Dupont sighed.

"Your blatant disregard for authority and reckless behaviour has already cost you your command and the lives of more than a few of the soldiers you had a responsibility to."

Taylor strode up to the bars quickly with a furious expression on his face. He had tried to remain calm during his imprisonment, but the French General made him sick.

"What the hell would you know about responsibility? You saw your country fall and sent armies to the slaughter!"

Dupont smiled with a wicked grin. It amused him that Taylor was behind bars. He could see the hatred that burned inside Taylor. Both men knew that Mitch wanted to tear the General apart. He turned and paced away from the door. He knew there was no way to air his frustration. He finally stopped and turned near his bed.

"At least tell me the status of my Company, and of Captain Jones."

"They are not your Company, Major. They are our Company, under the Joint European Command. The fact you could not get that into your head is the very reason you stand in that cell today."

"Please, General, just tell me how my people are."

"As a result of your actions, they have been removed from the Reiter programme, and they're out there doing their job."

"You mean they're getting fucked because of this."

"They are paid to do their job, which is to follow orders."

"What have you come here for, beyond torturing me with useless bullshit information?"

Taylor couldn't take it any longer. He'd longed to have someone to talk to, but Dupont was the last person he had in mind. He wondered if he'd ever get out of his cell, of if he'd be left to the mercy of the enemy like Jones was.

"General Schulz requested that you be officially informed of your status."

"What status? You're leaving me here to rot when there is a war to fight!"

Dupont smiled, turned and walked away from the Major. It infuriated Taylor that he still knew nothing more about his comrades. Dupont isn't a real soldier. He'd understand if he was, thought Taylor. He suddenly became overwhelmed by the thought of being left to the enemy. The gaunt body of Jones, and the empty look in his eyes, were burnt into Taylor's mind. He leapt to his feet and thrashed himself against the bars.

"Don't leave me down here, General! You need me!" he yelled.

He could just see the back of the General and the

guards as they continued to walk away, as if they had not even heard him. He smashed his hands against the cell bars in a desperate attempt get their attention, but it made little difference.

"Fuck!" he screamed.

Taylor knew that Dupont and Schulz were bastards, but he never imagined they would be so evil. Schulz is going to ruin the Company. God help them if any harm comes to Chandra and the others. He paced back to his bed and slumped down onto the hard and uncomfortable mattress. He felt utterly lost. Being locked up was bad enough, but knowing his friends were being led by such murderous bastards was too much to bear. This can't go on forever, I have to get out!

* * *

"Have you seen these co-ordinates, Captain?" asked Silva.

Friday looked up with a grim expression. He knew exactly the meaning of the Sergeant's query.

"We have our orders, Sergeant."

Silva took several quick steps to come up beside the Captain and out of earshot of the platoon who were checking and readying their equipment.

"A scouting party three clicks east for an engineering company to get to work, and two clicks back. We might as well walk towards their guns."

"Dupont wants us to start gaining ground and moving our positions forward. They will work under the cover of the main lines while we are there to give a heads up in case of any trouble."

"Sir, a few dozen of us with this old kit in no man's land. Tell me that isn't suicidal. Tell me this isn't a death sentence to punish us."

Friday knew that the Sergeant was right, but he also knew there was little to be done about it.

"What am I to do? We follow the chain of command."

"Major Taylor didn't," snapped Silva.

"And look where it got him."

Friday sighed. He hated his current position.

"Look, I am not saying what the Major did was wrong. I would have done the same in a heartbeat, but if we want to get him back, we need to pave the road for his return. Schulz is not beyond punishing all of us for a single deed."

Silva spat on the ground beside him. He was utterly disgusted by their leaders.

"Why the fuck are we fighting for such assholes?"

Friday continued to check his weapon over and answer the question as the Sergeant became angrier. His heavy breathing over the Captain finally forced Friday to look up and answer.

"We aren't fighting for them, Sergeant. We are fighting for ourselves, and for each other and every poor bastard on this world who can't fight for themselves. The masses wouldn't stand a chance. So we have to deal with obnoxious Generals. How is that any different to any other period in our history? There are some damn fine officers in this army and some damn bad ones."

"Army, thought we were marines, Sir?"

"We are whatever we need to be. We live in the most uncertain times that anyone has ever known. We can keep fighting against each other, or we can move forward to take the fight to the invaders. The time will come when the brass will remember how much they need Taylor."

Silva nodded as he took in what the Captain was saying. He had let his anger over the Major's detainment cloud his judgement and deter him from the tasks at hand. Friday could see in Silva's face that the Sergeant was beginning to come to his senses.

"You have been the best NCO I have had the pleasure of serving with, Sergeant. Your cool headedness and efficiency has kept us alive through the worst of it. Stay the course. Do exactly as you have been doing, and we'll be fine, as will the Major."

"Yes, Sir," he replied.

Friday could see some relief in the Sergeant's face. His shoulders relaxed slightly, and he had calmed substantially. Friday was just as frustrated at the Major's imprisonment as any of them. They had been best of friends from just a few months after enlistment. A German soldier rushed up and stopped to speak with the Captain.

"Sir, the engineers are ready to move forward, ready when you are."

Friday turned to Silva.

"Be sure the platoon is ready to leave, Sergeant. We go in five."

* * *

"Ma'am, is it correct that Captain Friday has been sent out over the top?" asked Yorath.

She nodded with a sullen and begrudging expression.

"Did his platoon get the Reitech gear issued?"

Chandra shook her head.

"What? They were sent out there with fuck all? No armour, no decent gear. Who the hell gave that order?"

She continued to look out into the ruined wastelands that stood between their lines and the enemy.

"This is yet more punishment isn't it? Schulz can't get over Major Taylor's rescue mission?"

"I thought that much was clear weeks ago, Lieutenant," she replied.

"Fuck sake. When is he going to start thinking like a soldier and not like a selfish bastard?"

She smiled. It amused her that the young officer was surprised at the General's response.

"How could it ever have been any different, just because Taylor did the right thing? There are consequences to every action. Taylor knew that, as did we all. I will happily pay any price Schulz can levy at us, in knowing that we left no one behind."

"If only I could get my hands on that bastard! Taylor should be running this army. We'd be half way across France by now."

Chandra turned in surprise.

"Careful what you say, Lieutenant. Even the suggestion of such could be enough to warrant you a cell opposite the Major."

"Fuck it, I don't care anymore. We have done nothing but our very finest to fight this enemy. We have given everything, and Taylor more than anyone. How can anyone lock him away now? This army needs him!"

Chandra said nothing and continued to stare into the distance. The plain before them was largely flattened by the weeks of brutal combat. The twisted wrecks of armoured vehicles of both sides littered the ground and fallen burnt trees lay among them. Finally, she turned to Yorath with a smile.

"You've still got me, Lieutenant."

* * *

Friday advanced cautiously across the uneven ground. The shelling of the area had created huge craters in the terrain. They made slow progress weaving in and out of debris and clambering up and over the ruined fields. The German engineer crews had already got to work behind them. They could make out other similar scouting parties far off in the distance.

"The General must be trying to advance the whole line," whispered Silva.

"You didn't think it was just us, did you?" replied Friday.

Silva smiled. They both assumed they'd been given a uniquely shit mission.

"Nice to know we aren't the only ones on the shit list, hey?" Silva jested.

They continued onwards as ordered through the rubble of no man's land until they could no longer see the other scouting parties on their flanks. The barren wasteland that had been the battleground for Ramstein was over two kilometres wide. The humans recovered their wounded where possible, but the Mechs seemed to care little for their casualties.

The bodies of the invaders were scattered across the ruined land amongst torn apart vehicles. The heavy artillery on either side had reduced much of what attempted to cross it to little more than shrapnel. A few metres away, Captain Friday could see a French soldier's helmet and half of a weapon, but there was little sign of any body.

"Jesus, this place is like a fucking scrap yard," whispered Silva.

The cool wind had carried away much of the foul stench

that had inhabited the battlefield, but it couldn't make the air fresh or barely more than tolerable. Silva could see a Mech that had been torn in half and bled out while still in its armour. Its blue blood had dried and hardened to an almost black oily texture.

The soldiers had been through hell, but never had they inhabited the same battlefield for such a prolonged period. They hadn't ever had to awaken to the sight of sheer destruction every morning. Friday caught the sound of a craft darting across the sky, and he looked up in surprise to see a small plane flash across at high speed. He could just make out the shape as a Eurofighter XB. A split second later, an enemy fighter blasted past on its tail.

Friday and several of the other marines looked up to see the enemy fighter fire on the XB and blast it out of the sky. Just seconds later, the sky erupted with anti-aircraft fire and punched gaping holes in the enemy fighter. It plummeted to the ground in a burning rage. Friday shook his head in sadness. He knew the German plane would have been gathering essential information.

"You can't doubt their courage," said Silva.

Friday nodded in agreement. The air war had become an unusual occurrence in the last week, as if both sides had simply lost too many craft or pilots to keep up the effort.

"I guess it's down to us to slug it out now, like we always have," mused the Sergeant.

"Let's move out," replied Friday.

It was a sad sight to see one of their planes brought down. The Captain could already feel his platoon had taken a knock to their morale, which was already low since being ordered on their mission. Up ahead, they could see the forest growing nearer; they hadn't got that near in weeks. They'd watched the tree lines with a keen eye every day, wondering what lay beyond them.

Friday was suspicious as they approached, more so than should be expected. He knew the enemy positions lay some way ahead, but the utter tranquillity made him nervous.

"Keep alert," he whispered.

The platoon's pace slowed as they closed the distance until they reached the rim of the forest. Friday was astonished they'd made it without incident, and a fact which made him all the more suspicious.

"Fan out, we hold here for twenty minutes."

"Sir, aren't we supposed to be scouting these woods?" asked Silva.

"Walking around until we find trouble? Fuck that, I'm not getting any of these troops killed because some General has a gripe."

Silva smiled. He knew Friday always had their best interests at heart. The Captain was like the little brother of Major Taylor. He had all the strength, courage and leadership of their former leader. They lay in wait for the twenty minutes, but it felt more like half the day. Finally, Friday stood up and stretched his aching knees, leaning over to Silva.

"Pass the word. We head north along the forest edge, three metre spacing."

A minute later, the platoon arose and continued their trek onwards. Just five minutes after they had set off, a volley of light pulses flashed through the trees to their west. Friday had just enough time to shout before the impacts struck.

"Incoming!"

Friday and Silva hit the ground as the first pulses erupted. The three above them burst with an ear-splitting explosion, sending foliage smashing down over their bodies. Friday's head was smashed into the mud by the weight of a falling branch. Only his helmet and the soft ground saved him from being crushed.

He shrugged off the branch and turned in the mud to see the status of the platoon, as fire continued to rain down on their heads. He could make out the body of one dead private already, and could only imagine the injuries he couldn't see from his position. He could hear screams of pain and calls for the medic running down the line, but they were going unanswered.

The Captain got up onto one knee while huddling behind a thick three trunk to get a better view of their surroundings. He could see at least a dozen Mechs firing on their position and knew there would be more closely behind. He turned back to Silva and bellowed his orders.

"Fall back. Fighting withdrawal!"

Silva nodded and quickly relayed the command at twice the volume the Captain could manage. The two men got to their feet and quickly returned fire with their weapons. The ineffectiveness of their old battle rifles was a painful experience after living Reiter's weaponry. Friday hit one of the Mechs with eight shots to the faceplate but did not penetrate. He ducked back behind cover, firing another burst into the same target zone and finally broke through, killing the creature immediately.

Now in a standing position, he could fully see the damage around them. There was only one dead marine but five wounded.

"Get those wounded out of here now!"

Several of the platoon rushed to the aid of their fallen comrades, hauling them onto their shoulders and beating a hasty retreat. Friday turned back around to train his rifle on another target but realised that a pulse was soaring towards him.

"Captain!" shouted Silva.

It was too late. The pulse smashed into Friday's chest and blew a hole through his torso. Silva could only watch in despair as the officer's body went limp and tumbled to the ground. He watched for only a second and turned to the platoon, repeating the Captain's orders. He rushed forward to Friday's body. He prayed the Captain had survived, but he already knew there was no hope.

Smoke rose from Friday's webbing where it had been burnt by the pulse. He turned the Captain over to see the last light in his eyes fade before he could get out his last words.

"Fuck!" Silva shouted.

He got up, hauling Friday's body onto his shoulder as if it was nothing at all. His hatred of the enemy would not allow him to leave the body of their Captain at the mercy of the enemy. He turned and rushed from the scene at a jogging pace. As he ran, he could see a number of the marines turning and giving covering fire.

"Forget it! Run! Run!"

Seeing the body of their officer across Silva's shoulders, they didn't need much encouragement to follow their Sergeant in fleeing outright. They had done little that day and were full of energy. The platoon scarpered across the rough terrain of no man's land, knowing their lives depended on it. After half a kilometre, the Sergeant finally stopped and looked back. He'd noticed the enemy guns had stopped firing. Corporal Hall rushed up beside Silva and turned to investigate what he was glaring at.

"They've stopped?" he asked.

"They know it's suicide to cross those lines, just as we knew it."

"Then why the fuck are we out here?"

Silva shook his head in astonishment.

"Two fine marines were thrown away because of one man's attitude problem. I'll be damned if I'll let there be another."

Hall nodded in agreement.

"This shit has got to end. We have to get back into the fight for real, and we need our gear back. We need our Major back!"

CHAPTER FIVE

"What the hell is going on out there?" shouted Chandra.

The troops around her said nothing. They could all tell that the mission had gone sour. She stared out across the plain, looking with her binoculars for any sign of the platoon, but they had long ducked and weaved their way out of her sight. She spun around with a furious expression. Her heart was heavy, but she could only imagine at the losses.

"Major!" shouted Blinker.

The Private came frantically rushing across the tops of the trenches to reach Chandra.

"What is it, Private?"

"Ma'am, you'd better come with me."

She stepped forward and grabbed the soldier back by the collar of his shirt, hauling him in close.

"Tell me what the fuck is going on!"

Blinker gasped to find his words but could not answer. Monty arrived a few metres behind his brother, and Chandra turned her gaze to the soldier. She could see the same blank expression on the man's face. She released her grasp and looked at their bleak pale faces.

"Please, Major, come with us," whispered Blinker.

She knew it was not the time to press the two brothers. Chandra nodded in agreement.

"Alright, lead on."

The Major knew that whatever she was about to witness was not good news, but she tried not to jump to any conclusions. Ten minutes later they reached a troop staging area just a hundred metres from the front line trenches. She recognised a few of Friday's platoon, but the Captain was nowhere to be seen. The two brothers led her on through a mix of allied troops into an opening where a doctor was overseeing a wounded marine being taken off on a stretcher.

Blinker turned and continued onwards. The wounded man was clearly not what he was bringing her for. Then she saw it, the bodies of two marines laid out flat on the ground. Sergeant Silva was sitting on an ammunition box a couple of metres away with his head in his hands. She looked down at the bodies and instantly recognised Friday, but she didn't want to believe it. Chandra took a few paces closer so she could get a better look at the face to be certain.

She shook her head as she realised beyond any doubt that it was Captain Friday. A gaping hole had been torn through his chest. The light armour they wore had done little to slow the path of the energy pulse. Little blood seeped from the Captain's body due to the immense heat at which the round had struck. It was clear to her that he had died within seconds.

The sight of Friday's body reminded her of her own mortality. She had thrown herself into the most brutal and prolonged combat with little care in the world. Now she was starting to appreciate life more. She looked at the faces of the troops around her. Many stared in astonishment that the Captain had fallen, and others looked away and hoped to forget. She had known Friday long enough to consider him a good friend, but it was clear that to the marines he was far more than that.

"Taylor should know," said Monty.

Chandra nodded. She already knew that the news would be monumentally tragic to Taylor who was closer to Friday than any of them. Having lost Jones in Amiens, she knew to some extent how he would feel. But at least at that time she still had some hope of Jones' survival; there was no coming back for Friday.

"You think this will be enough to warrant a pass to see the Major?" asked Blinker.

"It's sad to think that's what it could take, but you might be right," she fumed.

She stepped over and knelt beside Silva who looked more lost than the rest. He was an astonishingly tough and capable man, but it had been too much to bear. As she lowered herself down onto one knee, he looked up at her with a distraught expression.

"He didn't stand a chance," muttered Silva.

"You were ordered out there alone? No support? No armour?" she asked.

Silva nodded as he came close to tears.

"You did right by your platoon, Sergeant. You got them out," she whispered.

"When will it all end, Major? How many friends do we have to lose?"

Chandra shook her head. It was a question she had been asking herself since a few days after the war had begun. Death and dismemberment had become a part of their everyday lives, but it never got any easier to accept.

"We may be asked to give all of our lives before this is over, Sergeant. Would that be so bad? Us dying, in place of those who cannot fight for themselves, and the millions who do not stand a chance against these creatures."

She could see that Silva was starting to see some sense. He looked up to see the platoon was at an all time low point, and that they all looked to him.

"Look at the good we have done. How many of those bastards have we killed and left in our wake? Together, we cannot be stopped. We are the Immortals, and remember that. Remember how many soldiers rely on us for inspiration."

Silva nodded. He knew in his heart that the Major was right. He knew he was the one who should be giving such words of encouragement to the demoralised platoon. He could see that their shell shock and depression was already starting to rub off on the other members of the Company around them. He leaned in closer to the Major.

"We are stronger together. Get Taylor back," he whispered.

Silva leaned back and stood up with a newfound confidence and strength. He drew in a deep breath to bellow his words to the demoralised marines. Just as he was about to speak, he was interrupted by a vehicle's horn blaring as the driver made his way through the surrounding troops. He looked to identify the incoming vehicle that was clearly trying to reach them with some urgency.

As the troops scattered, and the vehicle came in to view, they could make out the HQ stencils and realised that General Schulz sat in the back.

"Fuck," muttered Silva under his breath.

Chandra's back straightened as she saw the General she resented so much. He sat confidently in the back of the vehicle, as if to be welcomed and celebrated by the front line troops he had been sending to their deaths. He peered around at the joint allied units in surprise at the cold response he was getting. The jeep pulled up just a few metres from Chandra and the body of Captain Friday that still lay uncovered.

Schulz stepped out from his vehicle and looked around at the stone cold faces around them. He looked down to see the dead Captain and the horrific chest wound which was on display for all to see. He made a quick scan of the pips of his uniform that marked Friday out as an officer.

"Major! Why has the body of this Captain not been covered?"

Schulz's tone was arrogant and lacked any understanding of the situation. Chandra did not respond, knowing she could do little to make him change his mind. Schulz turned to the nearest marine.

"You, find something to cover the body of this officer, immediately!"

The marine hesitated, as if he wasn't sure whether to carry out the order or not. The very possibility of such infuriated the General.

"Now, Private!"

"Hold that order!" bellowed Chandra.

Schulz's piercing eyes turned on the Major. He was taken aback by her comments, even more than the Private's hesitation to carry out his orders. It left him so speechless that Chandra seized the opportunity to carry on before he could condemn her.

"Captain Friday is one of our own. He has been with us through the worst of this war, and he is not left there out of ill discipline or idleness. He is there for all to see and pay their respects. As you are well aware, General, there is little time for proper burials in this life anymore. This is the only time we have to pay our final respects."

The General's expression did not change, but he slowly breathed out and calmed himself. He looked around at the faces of the troops. He could tell that many had been with Friday when he was killed, and they looked down on the General with disgust that he would try and interfere.

Chandra knew the General had put Friday and his men in harm's way. The rest of the troops did too, but they all knew it was not wise to anger the General. She could hear Silva's knuckles crunch as he clenched his fists. He wanted to strike the General more than any of them, but he didn't move a millimetre. Schulz coughed and cleared his throat. He had quickly realised it was not the time or place to risk angering the already distraught troops. He was also well aware that soldiers from many armies were watching. They were eyes and ears that could lead to his downfall if he made the wrong move.

Major Chandra could tell that Schulz's arrogance had led him into a vulnerable position, and it was one that she was all too ready to take advantage of. She stepped forward and squared off against the General. Her body language could have been read as either respectful or challenging, and she revelled in the fact that he could not tell which.

"Sir, Captain Friday was a brave and competent officer

in my Company, and whose actions have saved the lives of many. He was selfless in life, and loyal and honest to the end. Friday was a marine under the direct command of Major Taylor, as well as a very close friend. As the commanding officer of both men, I request a visitation to Major Taylor in order to pass on this tragic news."

She could see the fury in Schulz's eyes. The German General hated the insolence he had witnessed with the Inter-Allied Company that she led. Yet he had no choice but to accept her presence whilst she remained a competent and honest officer. He had done his utmost to keep Taylor isolated from any of the personnel he had served with. Schulz had already realised that few who came into contact with the Major would not be sympathetic to his situation and actions.

Schulz turned slowly in a full circle and looked for some indication of what to do. Chandra could tell he was not looking out of concern for the troops, but to find out how he could come off best in the situation. Most of the soldiers glared at him. They despised Schulz for taking Taylor away from them, and not one of them accepted that Taylor had done a thing wrong. Even more so, they hated Schulz for abandoning POWs.

The General nodded as he turned. He was quickly realising that he had to do something to alleviate the situation. The anger and hatred surrounding him made him wonder if the marines would set on him if he didn't say what they wanted to hear. He licked his lips and readied himself to speak loudly and clearly. Schulz wanted to come off as the hero, but it rarely worked.

"I am deeply saddened by the loss of your Captain..."

"Friday," muttered Silva.

Schulz turned and nodded at the Sergeant, as if thanking him. Silva was well aware that Schulz didn't appreciated being interrupted, but he could do little in response without losing the respect of everyone present.

"Captain Friday was a good soldier and a good man. He has fought to defend lands that were not his and helped save the lives of millions of civilians who he had never known. We are thankful for his service and his sacrifice. May we all be remembered for such great deeds and unwavering gallantry."

Chandra looked down in disgust. Bastard, he doesn't give a shit, she thought. Schulz stopped and looked to the troops to judge their reaction. They didn't look impressed, and he knew he had to give them more if he was to come off well in the situation. Chandra once again seized the moment.

"Sir, the one thing Friday would want more than anything would have been to know that Major Taylor is alright. This news will hit Taylor hard. May I again request permission to see the Major and relay this news?"

Schulz smirked just a little as he thought about how he had been played by Chandra. She had chosen her moment well, and it was clear that he couldn't refuse her without having a detrimental effect on all those around them, and perhaps the armies at large. Chandra revelled for just a moment in how she had managed to manipulate. Her smile faded as she thought about the Captain who had so recently fallen. Schulz finally nodded in agreement.

"Very well. Captain Friday gave his life in the service of this army, and you may carry that news to Major Taylor. Send my deepest sympathies for the loss of his friend."

The Major watched as Schulz made a final scan of the troops. He was desperately looking for any sign of respect, but it was barely in evidence. He could tell he had narrowly missed all out violence. Now piss off, thought Chandra. Finally, the General stepped back into his vehicle, and many of the troops watched in disgust as his driver pulled away. They looked back down to the body of Friday and the other marine. Medical orderlies waited to take the bodies away but were loathed to interfere.

"Alright, that's enough! Captain Friday is gone, and another fine soldier taken from us in this war. He was exceptional in life and will remain so in our memories long after death. We have a war to fight. Friday knew that, so let's get on with it!"

She nodded for the medics to come forward and spirit the bodies away. She could already hear the mutinous mutterings from a number of the marines who had been with Friday on his mission. They all knew that his death had been a direct result of Taylor's rescue mission.

"How the fuck can this go on?" asked Hall. "We came here to help, and we're getting fucked over because some General was made to look an idiot!"

"Careful, Corporal. You are under the General's command, and you must show him respect."

"Why on Earth should we? He's abandoned our people, locked up the Major and continues to put us in danger without the equipment we need. Why on Earth are we fighting for that asshole?"

"We aren't fighting for him. We're fighting for us." She pointed out at the other troops surrounding them. "And for them. Yes, Schulz is a bastard, but that's nothing new. Right now, the only thing you should be concerned about is getting Taylor and our gear back. Pissing off the General further, isn't the way to do it."

Hall slumped down onto a supply box. He knew he was not helping the situation, but he couldn't help venting his anger. He remembered the surge of relief and fulfilment when he was stood beside Taylor as they found and rescued the POWs. Never could he have imagined they could be punished so severely for doing what had been drilled into them, to leave no man behind.

"Take some rest, get cleaned up and get some chow. I have a chance to see Taylor here, and that's the best progress we have seen since all this shit started. Sergeant Silva! You are in charge of the platoon until instructed otherwise."

Silva accepted without a word. They were large shoes to fill, but he was the only soldier up to the task. The marines had been diminished to such low numbers, and with few officers left between them. Lieutenant Suarez was a hot tempered and self-centred officer, but at least he had made it this far. Chandra would far rather see Silva promoted over him, but it was a political move that would cause more trouble than she needed. She paced up closely to the Sergeant who still stood with a sombre face.

"These marines need you more than ever. You are what can make the difference in holding them together. We have a long way to go in this war, so let's continue to deserve our reputation. Get them rested, and do whatever you have to," she whispered.

Silva took a step back, and his wary expression turned quickly to the competent and sharp keen eyed Sergeant she had come to know.

"Say hi to the Major for us, Ma'am, and let him know we expect his return quickly."

"I'll pass on your comments, Sergeant."

"Good luck, Ma'am."

Chandra nodded in gratitude. Although she had little faith in Suarez's leadership, she knew Silva was well up to the task of pulling the marines out of the hole they were in. She took one last look at Friday's body as it was carried away and turned to leave the staging area. What a fucking mess, she thought.

* * *

Taylor ate slowly from a bowl of food that he couldn't even name. It was a prison blend of key ingredients that the human body needed. It was a mush that no one would eat if not to avoid starving. As an officer, he was entitled to far better provisions, but he knew that Schulz or Dupont would have seen to that being restricted.

Keeping his strength up was always on his mind. He ate whatever was put before him and exercised regularly in his cell. The Major hoped to get out every day and knew that he needed to be combat ready the second it happened. As the weeks passed, he wondered if he would ever get out. General White would have procured his release, but he knew that the US was too busy fighting on its own soil.

Is White even still alive? thought Taylor. He had heard no news since being detained. All he knew was that Ramstein had held against the enemy attacks. It was a fact that both pleased and dismayed the Major. Holding for such time was a huge boost for the human forces. But had it fallen, he would have seen the light of day.

Where are you Eli? Where is my Company?"

Mitch had been going crazy locked up in the cell. He'd never expected being imprisoned would be pleasant, but when his friends were fighting and dying just kilometres away, it was the most painstaking experience. He hoped to see a familiar face from his Company every hour of every day. Instead, all he saw were the straight-faced guards and the sour Dupont.

As Taylor took down another mouthful of the foul food, the doors down the corridor slid open. It was too early to be taking back the bowls, and not a likely time to be interning a new prisoner. He put his bowl down on the bed and stood up in curiosity. Three sets of footsteps strode down the hall towards his cell. Can't be Dupont, he's never without his paper pusher.

Taylor tensed up and froze in anticipation that he might see a friendly face. Then she appeared before him in a dreamy moment. He felt all hopelessness fade away as he saw Chandra's face. He was as much relieved to see she was still alive, as he was that she had not given up on him. The guards stopped at his cell with the Major between them.

"You've got five minutes," one of them snarled.

The guards strode off back down the corridor. They had not opened the doors to his cell. They never extended any courtesy to Taylor. It made him wonder how on earth Chandra managed to get in, but his moment of joy faded as he saw the sombre tone in her face. He leapt forward to the cell bars.

"I thought you'd forgotten me," he cried.

"Never! But you're at the top of Schulz's shit list, and

I've been through hell trying to get some contact with you."

"What finally made him sway?"

She looked down gravely before finally meeting Taylor's eyes once again. He had a thousand questions, but there were few she didn't want to answer. She realised she had no choice but to explain all their woes, even though it could destroy the Major's resolve.

"Since your imprisonment, we have been hit hard. Stripped of our equipment and thrown onto the front line. It's taken a heavy toll. Schulz has had us out on suicidal missions, and more than our fair share."

"What are you trying to tell me, Major?" insisted Taylor.

She sighed as she tried to find the words to explain.

"One of our platoons was ordered forward today, to go beyond no man's land and scout ahead of an engineer party. That platoon was led by Captain Friday. Several hours into the mission, they were attacked in the heavy woodland on the western side, and Friday was struck in the fight."

"And, is he okay?"

Taylor thought back to the early days of the war, and how little protection they had against the enemy energy weapons. His face turned to dread as it became clear what she was saying.

"I am sorry to say that Captain Friday died of his wounds during the firefight, along with Private Rollings."

Taylor turned and gasped in shock. He stopped breathing for a few seconds as he stared at the back wall of his cell. Shortly after, his shock turned to anger, and he rushed back at the cell bars and threw his body against them.

"Why? Why the fuck, am I still in here? This is Schulz's doing!"

Chandra looked in despair at Mitch's furious anger.

"Tell me it wasn't those two bastard Generals who caused this!"

She shook her head, not able to contradict him.

"They could have sent anyone out there. Someone had to do it, and that someone was Friday," stated Chandra.

"Fuck!" he screamed. "Those bastards are going to pay for this!"

"Ultimately, it was the enemy that killed Friday. It was the Krycenaeans that started this war. It was them who killed our friends and brought this destruction to our world. We can do nothing to Schulz and Dupont, but if we can get you out, then you can get some payback against those alien bastards."

Taylor strode forward more calmly, leaned in against the bars and dipped his head. He squeezed the bars with a strong clenched grip, trying to release some of his anger.

"That is what they are called? Krycenaeans?" he muttered.

"Yes. Since you rescued Jones, we have learnt a few

things about our enemy. That is what they call themselves."

Taylor's sullen tone suddenly lifted slightly.

"Charlie? How is he?"

"I have only seen him a couple of times. He's been taken to a recovery facility further east. Honestly? He's a wreck. Whatever they did to him... well, he may never recover."

"Jesus, we're dropping like flies. Have you been reinforced?"

Chandra shook her head. She couldn't believe it either.

"What? Who are your platoon leaders?"

"Yorath, Suarez and now Silva. Green was wounded a week ago."

Taylor sighed.

"What is the fighting strength of the Company?"

She did not respond.

He looked up and stared into her eyes. He could see it was an answer she didn't want to give. He glared until finally she folded.

"Sixty-five at present."

"And your people won't send any fresh troops?"

"British forces are already fighting further north of here. They arrived last week. There is still speculation of a new front being started in Northern France."

"They're going to tackle the Normandy beaches? Jesus!"

"We all hope it'll happen, but I guess they need to know there's a good chance of success. It's not like we have anywhere to run if Britain falls."

Taylor paced up and down the room. He was glad to finally be getting some news, but it made him all the more furious that he was locked up and unable to help his comrades.

"You have to get me out of here!"

"I am well aware of that, but what am I supposed to do?"

"Anything! Everything!"

"I'm doing everything in my power to make it happen, but you'll just have to wait. The war rages on, but the front line has reached a stalemate. At the moment, nobody is inclined to look at your case."

"You think we have broken their momentum?"

"It certainly looks that way, but I'd hate to jump to conclusions. We have underestimated them more than once before at a terrible cost," she replied.

"What am I going to do? I'm going fucking crazy in here. I'm a marine, and I am here to fight."

"There's nothing you can do. I'll keep pushing and see if I can at least see you again soon. You'll be needed before long, so hold on."

Taylor's face was bleak. She could see the weeks of isolation had taken a lot from him, and it pained her that she had nothing but bad news to convey. The guards appeared at the end of the corridor striding quickly towards her.

"Time's up!"

She looked back to Taylor, trying to think of some last words of comfort.

"Thank you."

"For what?"

"For getting through to me. I know it can't have been easy."

"The Company needs you, Major. The world needs you. Without soldiers like you, we are lost. You hold out and stay strong."

The guards formed up beside her and led her out of the prison, as Taylor watched the only friend he had seen in weeks disappear once again. Seeing her face had given him hope, but having spoken to her, he realised how bad his situation was. He lay back down on the bed, the only luxury he was provided, and slipped into a dream.

Friday had been one of Taylor's best friends. In war and peace, they had always stood together. He had always thought that if they were to fall, it would be together. That night his dreams turned to nightmares as he pictured how the Captain had died based on Chandra's description. The same images plagued him night after night until he lost track of time.

Each day he pushed his body harder, as he had little else to do but find new and creative ways to exercise in the small cell that had become his home. The only relief was not to be in a wet trench in the cold nights, but he'd give up the relative comfort and warmth to be among his

BATTLE EARTH III

comrades once again in a second. He woke up every night in sweats as his mind was filled with scenes of death and destruction.

He'd seen countless friends killed and heard of many more meeting the same fate. Then his mind slipped to the mounds of bodies he'd seen at the prison when they rescued Jones and the others. He wondered what could bring any race to such cruelty and slaughter. The human race had moved past it, so how could such a technologically advanced race still be stuck in such primitive ways?

* * *

Silva slumped down at a canteen table. Command had pushed hard to ensure they had good food to keep their morale up, but it went unnoticed by the Sergeant. He had to keep up a brave and confident persona around the Company, but it was taking its toll on him. He'd not ever dreamed to see the kind of vast scale death and war that his ancestors had. Reading about such conflicts had been a pleasure. He'd wished to be given the opportunity to gain the glory and respect they had earned.

Parker and Hall leapt onto the bench opposite his table. He looked up at them and smiled as best he could, but they too looked beaten. They each looked to one another for some answers to make them feel better, but they didn't come.

"Shame to see Friday go. He was a good man."

Silva nodded at Parker.

"They all were, every god damn man and woman in this Company," he muttered.

"I hear Chandra got a pass to see Taylor?"

Silva glared at her. For a moment he was irritated by her selfish hounding so soon after the death of one of their friends. But then he settled, realising just how much concern she had for the Major. He knew they could lose Taylor for good.

"She got it alright, and it wasn't an easy feat. She chose her moment carefully. Our boys were ready to tear Schulz apart."

"Should have let us," snapped Hall.

Silva sighed and shook his head in dismay.

"So you could all share a prison cell with Taylor?"

"Something has to be done. We can't leave him there to rot while we get sent out to die on pointless missions," replied Parker.

Silva smashed his hand down on the table, causing it to shake violently and several nearby troops turn and look. He gazed around at them until they looked away. He turned his attention back to the two marines.

"I've had enough of this bitching and whining. Taylor shouldn't be locked away, but there is nothing we can do about it. The morale has been shit since that time, and there is no excuse for it. That morale could get many more of us killed. Do you think Taylor would want that? Or do you think he'd want us to pick ourselves the fuck up and continue in his stead?"

The two NCOs looked sheepishly down at their food. Silva had successfully shamed them, but he didn't feel good about it.

"I know we need the Major back. Parker, you think you need him more than any of us, but you don't. We all need him back, and when the time comes, we will make it happen. But until that time, we act like god damn professionals and are ready for anything."

Parker looked up with a doleful face.

"You really think we'll get him back?"

"Fuck, yes. You hold onto that knowledge, and you carry it in battle with you. He's getting out, and he wants us there to greet him when it happens."

* * *

Three weeks had passed since the news of Friday's death. Taylor hadn't seen anyone but the guards in all that time. He prayed to see Dupont again, so he could vent his anger if nothing else. He knew Chandra and the others were doing everything in their power to help him, but he also knew what bastards Schulz and Dupont were.

He closed his eyes and thought back to his nights with Eli back before the war had started. Their sneaking around seemed dangerous at the time, but now it felt little more than harmless mischief. Everyday, he tried to think of her to stop his imagination taking him back the horrors he'd witnessed or been told of.

Then his mind swayed back to Friday. He remembered the first time they met early in their careers, and how competitive they had been. Within months, they had become like brothers and remained so through their service. The only friend who could come close was Jones. It pained him to know that he could do nothing for Friday, and he couldn't even attend his funeral. But it pained him even further that Jones had been left to become a hollowed out wreck.

Charlie's absent staring eyes came back into Taylor's mind. It frightened him that such a strong man could be reduced to such a lifeless state. With the loss of Friday, he held onto the fact that Jones was still alive, praying that he could return to the lively and joyful friend he used to know. As his mind crept to darker places, and he began to mutter to himself once again, the corridor doors opened and footsteps strode towards him. He jumped up out of bed and stood anxiously waiting to see a familiar face.

Chandra appeared before him once again with a smile on her alluring face. It was the most beautiful thing he had seen in recent memory, and instantly painted a picture of Eli in his mind.

"Come to get me out, Major?" he asked.

She shook her head.

"Sorry, but I have at least managed this, five minutes, once a week outside my duty hours."

"That's generous of the General," Taylor spat sarcastically.

She grinned at his sharpness. It pleased her to know he hadn't been beaten by his detainment. He was still the strong and sharp officer he always had been.

"No chance of me getting out, then?"

She shook her head and looked in with sympathy.

"No. I have tried everything I can. Anyone who could help with procuring your release is out of contact, fighting their own battles."

"So what you're saying is, unless a bomb happened to drop on the two Generals, I am not getting free?"

"That about sums it up. But for all of their hatred of you, they also know how useful you can be. There will come a time when they need you."

"How is the Company holding up?"

Locked up for months and still putting his friends first, she thought. Taylor never ceased to amaze her. She could only hope to have his strength if she had to endure the same.

"They're holding. The fighting has hit a lull. There continues to be skirmishes along the lines, but nothing like the onslaught we have become used to. It's given everyone a little time to rest and recover, but also more time to dwell on how shit the situation is."

"Any plan for an advance east?"

"Even if I were given access to such information, I'd never be allowed to share it with you in here," she warned.

The two went silent for a moment as they listened to the guards' footsteps trail off into the distance. Taylor dipped his head and thought before finally looking up and pleading with the Major.

"You promise me one thing. If those alien bastards push through this base, you won't leave me here. Not like Jones was."

She could see the despair in his face. She had never been able to fully comprehend what he had seen the day of Jones' rescue, and the state he had found the Captain in.

"There's no way in hell I am leaving anyone else behind. You can count on that."

"Thank you," whispered Taylor.

She could tell that it was the only fear Taylor had in life, and being behind bars made it all the worse.

"You hold on, Mitch. I'm getting you out of here, one way or the other. That's a promise, too."

The ground rocked beneath their feet as a huge artillery shell landed outside the building. Taylor looked up in fear, and they both quickly jumped to the correct conclusion; the enemy was advancing. Further explosions erupted all around the base that were deafening even through the thick walls. The guards came rushing down the corridor.

"Major Chandra! You are to report back to your unit immediately!"

"What the fuck is going on?"

"The enemy, they've launched a massive attack at our lines!"

"Jesus Christ!"

The guards grabbed the Major and started to lead her out. She strained to turn back to the Major and shout to him one last time.

"I'll come for you, Taylor!"

CHAPTER SIX

"Kelly! Kelly!" shouted Doyle.

The enthusiastic Private came charging down the dusty hallway into the storage room that was now their command centre. He was met with little positivity as the grim faces glared at him. Martinez turned to look at the furore. The Captain's face was badly scarred, and he wore a makeshift eye patch over his left eye. He had the look of a man who was awaiting his death with dignity.

Commander Kelly turned slowly around in his chair. He no longer expected good news and was therefore careful to gather up his hopes. He glared at the Private as if the cheery man had somehow broken the mood; a mood so miserable and dire that one might wish they were already dead. Doyle slid to attention before the two officers and made a quick and ill disciplined salute. He could barely contain himself and looked as if he was going to explode.

"What is it, Private?" insisted Kelly.

"They're leaving, Sir, by the bucket load!" he balled.

The room suddenly turned all attention on the excited man. For a moment, the people within it felt a spark of hope.

"What are you talking about?" asked Martinez with a doubtful tone.

Kelly leapt to his feet. He prayed for good news but knew it sounded too good to be true.

"Come on, Doyle, spit it out," Kelly shouted.

Doyle finally opened his mouth and blurted out his message.

"The enemy ships are leaving. Taking off all over the surface!"

The Commander spun around on the spot and turned to Lewis, who was sat at his makeshift console with cables hanging out all over the place, and multiple screens balanced across what furniture and mounts he could scavenge. Kelly didn't need to ask any questions. The communications officer was already slaving away at his station to corroborate Doyle's news that seemed unbelievable.

Several dozen soldiers waited silently for further news. They anxiously wanted to believe that Doyle was correct.

"Come on, come on..." whispered Martinez.

Lewis spun around in his chair and stared up at the Commander with a bewildered expression. For a moment he could not speak, and Kelly already knew the answer. A smile widened across his face before the man had even opened his mouth.

"He's right, Sir. They're leaving!"

A hail of excitement burst out as claps and whistles echoed around the room. Kelly took a few paces closer, so Lewis could hear him.

"Where are they going?"

Lewis turned back to his monitors and carefully studied the data. He swivelled back around in his chair with yet more surprise in his face.

"They're heading for Earth..."

Kelly smashed his hand down on the table rocking the consoles.

"Yes!" he screamed.

The deep booming roar from their Commander caused the room to go silent, and all attention to turn on him. Kelly could see new life in the eyes of all those around him. They had resigned themselves to fighting to the very last man and woman, but now there was hope.

"The enemy occupiers are departing for Earth. This can only mean one thing!" he bellowed.

Silence still filled the room. None of them had heard Lewis' last comment and had been too busy celebrating to care.

"They underestimated the human race! Earth forces are giving them hell, and they must be re-directing everything they have to get down there. The Earthers have given us an opportunity. Their blood and sacrifice may give us all the opening we need to take back our lands!"

Cheers rang out once again as further troops flooded in from the nearby corridors. Kelly turned back to Lewis who was mesmerised by the news.

"Lieutenant, open all channels."

Lewis stared at him in a daze for a moment, finally snapping out of it and turning back to his console. Seconds later, the Commander saw the lights fire up to signify an open channel.

"This is Commander Kelly. Alien forces are leaving our colony. We are not free of occupation. We still have a long way to go, but hope is once again with us. I repeat. Alien forces are leaving our colony in substantial number."

Rave applause echoed through the corridors as the colony's survivors burst into celebration. A Chinese officer rushed into the room with a broad smile on his face.

"Commander, has this news being verified?" he asked.

"Colonel Chen, we have just had visual confirmation. The tide just turned in this war."

"My Battalion is ready and awaiting your orders, Commander."

Kelly knew the Chinese troops were eager to get into action since they arrived the week before. They were the only soldiers to come to the aid of the Lunar colony since Taylor's mission to rescue the Prime Minister.

"Thank you, Colonel."

He turned back to the microphone to talk to the survivors of the colony.

"All units are to be ready for combat within the hour. Be patient, be strong, and be ready. The time is almost upon us to take back our homes, over and out."

He nodded for Lewis to stop the transmission and turned to Martinez and Chen. Martinez would never have liked giving up any authority or command to an Earth dweller, but now he would take any help he could get.

"I want to know those bastards have gone for good. I have no doubt they have left more than enough troops here to not make our life easy, so let's not get ahead of ourselves. As soon as we are confident that all who are going have left, and they are entering the Earth's atmosphere, it is our time to strike."

"You think we can do it this time?" asked Martinez.

"I think we have a damn good chance. We'll do this systematically. Corridor by corridor until we occupy all that is underground. I know we want the surface back, but we have to do it with caution."

"Agreed," replied Chen confidently.

"We are thankful of your support, Colonel, but you are likely to be the only help we see for some time, and we cannot afford to throw lives away. We paid a high price the last time we tried to move forward, so let's do this right. Both of you ready our troops. Remind them of what we are fighting for, and the price of failure."

* * *

"Go, go, go!" roared Chandra.

She could barely hear her own voice over the deafening explosions tearing through the base. She flinched as one struck a transport plane, and it burst into a thick ball of black smoke. Debris scattered across the ground between them and smashed into the rooftops of their billets. The Company rushed from their accommodation, desperately trying to pull on their equipment as they scurried out towards the trenches.

"So much for a rest!" shouted Hall.

"You can rest when you're dead, Corporal!" she barked.

Silva rushed to the Major's side with a look of bewilderment on his face. The troops of the Inter-Allied Company had been taking a much-needed spate of rest and had settled in for a few quiet card games and naps.

"What the fuck is going on, Major?" he hastily asked.

"The whole fucking Krycenaean army is advancing from Saarbrucken!"

"My God, then this wait was all about massing forces for a push?"

"Looks that way, follow my lead. We're heading for Gate B to the west, and we have to hold!"

"I don't see we have any other choice, Major," he replied

despondently.

She nodded with a pained grin and turned quickly, beckoning for the nearest troops to follow her. As she ran with her body held low, she could see troops and vehicles all over the base in an absolute frenzy, and as many were heading to the front line as were fleeing from it. She darted from building to building to cover the five hundred metres between them and the perimeter of the base.

Chandra could not see the front line through the scattered troops, vehicles and dust. As they grew nearer, she gained some visibility, gasping as she saw trees collapsing under the weight of the enemy tanks that were breaching the thick forest.

"Into the trenches now!" she cried.

They continued to rush forward as explosions burst all round them, and they felt the immense heat of the artillery pulses rush past. She sprinted across the open ground between the last of the buildings and the first trenches. The Major hoped her comrades were close behind, but she could no longer pause to think about it. She jumped and rolled into the closest trench, nearly knocking herself out as she landed hard in the floor beside a Russian officer.

The Company poured into the trenches all around her, squeezing in between those already huddled in for safety. Chandra shook her head to re-gain her senses and wiped the dust from her face as she looked to Silva.

"We can't stay here. We have to get our guns into

action!" she yelled.

"Not like we've got a lot that'll touch them, Major."

"That's life. We'll just have to hope someone else can do some of the work."

She looked at the troops around her. Their own Company were mixed in with two other units. They all looked as scared as each other. The last few weeks had made them complacent. They had gotten used to holding their ground and forgotten how terrifying their opponents could be.

"Let's move! On me!" ordered Chandra.

She clambered to her feet and followed the trench works further west. There were six layer of trenches constructed around the entire western perimeter of Ramstein. As they got closer to the front, they could hear the raucous grinding of the enemy tanks rumbling towards them. They were not stopped by any obstacles in the battered no man's land that had been fought over for so many weeks.

They finally reached the front line trenches, where German infantry were frantically trying to stop the oncoming tanks with what little heavy equipment they had. She didn't recognise any of the faces. With the tens of thousands of soldiers operating along the lines, it was rare for her to see anyone twice. She wondered how many of those she had stood beside in combat were now dead, but they were names she never knew.

"What the hell are we doing here, Major?" shouted

Blinker.

Chandra crawled up the side of the trench to look down the shallow slope towards the oncoming enemy. They were still a distance away and making slow but steady progress. Artillery shells whistled overhead and crashed down into the enemy advance. She watched as Mechs were tossed into the air like ragdolls and thrown back down into the mud. The pulse cannons on the tanks fired volleys into their positions, and dirt peppered the hunkered down troops. The Major looked down at the soldiers hiding from the enemy guns.

"Get the fuck up here and start shooting!" she yelled.

She lifted her rifle up onto the edge of trench and took careful aim at the first Mech that drew her attention. The armoured creature was still seven hundred metres out, but she had to feel that they were doing something. She aimed, squeezed the trigger and watched the round bounce off the Mech's faceplate.

"God damn it!"

She looked over at Sergeant Silva.

"We need our god damn weapons back!"

She watched as Campbell laid his huge anti-materiel rifle down and quickly took aim. He was careful to select the creature the armour had defiantly brushed off the Major's rifle. He quickly pulled the trigger, and she turned to see blood spew from the baseball-size hole in its facial armour. The beast went limp and smashed down into the dirt. She turned and nodded in appreciation to the marine sniper.

"Get the ARMALs up here, and anything else we have got!"

Mortars fired off in sequence in the trench behind them, sending further fire forwards. The big guns roared to the east in support. She could hear gunfire and pulse weapons raging for miles. They all knew the time had come. The enemy weren't stopped in their tracks weeks before, and they were only rallying their forces to smash the allied forces in Ramstein.

As the troops prepared what little heavy weaponry they had, the Major once again peered over the firing shelf to witness the fearsome advance. She could hear allied tanks rolling forward at their backs to join the fight. The sky lit up as an aerial strike began. She had just enough time to spot the multiple wings of enemy craft as the first pulses smashed into their positions. The vibrations threw her into the base of the trench. Lying flat on her back, the Major watched the enemy fighters rush past overhead with guns blazing.

"There's nothing left to stop them," stated Silva in a sombre tone.

They could hear the anti-aircraft weapons of the base blasting away, desperately trying to bring down the enemy craft, but their systems were woefully antiquated.

"We've lost the sky," muttered Chandra.

"Then be thankful we're bloody infantry!" shouted Silva.

"Not so much, we're the ones getting shit on!" yelled Blinker.

Chandra looked over to see the cheeky grin on the soldier's face. It astonished her that amid such a brutal bombardment and assault, he could keep his spirits high. It was enough to make her remember her job in it all. She rolled over onto her front and pushed herself up to her feet. Standing tall in the middle of the trench, she looked at the scared soldiers lining the walls.

"This war isn't going to fight itself! Do you want to wait here to be killed in this shithole, or give those bastards hell?" she cried.

Several of the beleaguered troops looked up at the Major. Her short stature never ceased to make her imposing.

"Come on, you bastards!"

They scrambled to the firing ledge and opened fire. The tiered trenches running down hill meant that gunfire flew over their heads from the allied units at their backs. Smoke plumes raced towards the enemy as the rockets soared towards them. Chandra knew their equipment was inadequate against the Krycenaean armour, but they could not lie down and do nothing.

Tracer fire lit up the battlefield, but it was overwhelmed by the vast energy pulses smashing into their positions.

No man's land was little more than a scrap heap and pile of rubble. Many of the craters were so large that the advancing tanks all but disappeared in the dips. A huge explosion rang out as one of them ran over an anti-tank mine. Chandra watched as the monstrous vehicle bounced a few centimetres off the ground but kept moving. Seconds later, it hit a second which finally blew the tracks off.

Further explosions sent earth blasting into the sky as the advancing infantry reached the minefield that had been laid. Soldiers across the trenches screamed out in celebration as Mech soldiers were blasted into the air. Chandra revelled in their destruction. The bloodshed of humans made her want to howl, but she cheered the slaughter of their enemies. The cheering died as massive explosions erupted around the trench works.

"They're still coming," cried Monty.

"They mean to roll over us," growled Silva.

"And they bloody will, if we don't get some damn support!"

The guns of the allied tanks roared at their backs, but it was not enough to slow the enemy progress. As they reached the effective range of grenades, the troops opened up with a hail of gunfire and explosives in a desperate attempt to halt the creatures. Chandra could make out hundreds of Mechs in their field of fire alone, and many more through the smoke to both the north and south.

"Major, we can't hold here!" shouted Silva.

"We have to!" she replied desperately.

The Mechs increased pace as they bounced along the rough terrain on their spring legged armour, approaching a jogging speed. She leapt up onto the trench and fired on full auto at the nearest, striking it with twenty rounds to the faceplate until it smashed down into the dirt. It slid a metre uphill with its momentum. The Mechs advancing towards them were smashed down by the heavy weapon fire and sustained weapons in the line, but it was not enough.

The surviving enemy Mechs rushed into the trenches and kept firing as they moved. Chandra saw a creature leap in just a few metres from where she was standing. It crushed one of the German infantrymen as it landed, obliterating another with its pulse cannon at close range. Screams of panic rang out across the lines as gunfire opened up inside the trenches.

Bullets bounced off the thick armour of the creature. It was almost impossible to get a fix on its weak points as it thrashed around the trench, firing and crushing soldiers as if they were toys. Four of the German soldiers were dead before Chandra could even respond, but Hall was already on his feet. He climbed out the back of the trench and rushed along the top.

"Aim for the head!" cried Chandra.

Hall reached the edge of the trench above the creature as it trained its cannon on a group of soldiers whose rifle

BATTLE EARTH III

fire was ricocheting off its armour. He lifted his rifle and opened up on full auto against the top of the creature's armoured suit. It spasmed sharply and smashed its cannon into the Corporal. Hall was launched into the air and tumbled back down to the ground hard. He rolled across the muddy surface until coming to a dead stop.

The Major turned to shout her orders but found Silva stood with an ARMAL launcher held at the hip. She leapt aside as he fired. Smoke filed the trench, and a split second later a huge explosion tore through it. Metal shrapnel burst across the area, hitting several of the troops. Chandra yelped in pain as a sliver of metal impeded into her left arm. She turned away as the heat from the explosion blasted past.

As the dust settled, the Major turned to look at the carnage in the trench. The Mech had been blown apart and scattered across the bodies of the four dead soldiers. Gunfire continued to rage in the nearby trenches, and artillery fire still roared overhead. Silva rushed to her side and quickly checked her wound.

"You okay, Major?" he yelled.

She nodded back but could not yet get any words out. Her eardrums had popped, and she was still in shock at the devastation. She turned and stumbled, slightly falling back against the wall of the trench. The Major could see the distraught faces of the troops around her. The war was taking them face-to-face with their enemy, and it wasn't a pretty sight.

"We don't get our gear back soon, and we are fucking goners," whispered Silva.

She climbed back up to look over the trench with Silva. The Mech forces lay in ruin, but they could see columns of the enemy in the distance and heading for them.

"That was just the beginning," said Silva. "Within a few hours, those armies are going to roll up these hills, and there will be nothing we can do about it."

"Alright, Sergeant, gather up any wounded and head back to re-supply."

"Re-supply what, ammunition that can barely touch those bastards? The launchers we got early on this war finally gave us a fighting chance, but now we may as well throw stones at them!"

She grabbed the Sergeant's webbing and hauled him in close.

"I am well aware of that, Sergeant, but what am I to do?"

"Whatever you have to! This isn't just about us. If our armies fall here, it could be the end of the war in Europe." He pointed to the line of tanks behind their positions, several of which were engulfed in flames. "That armour and artillery is all that is keeping them from running us into the ground, and how long do you think it can last?"

She looked back to see Captain Becker kneeling down beside one of the wounded tank crewmen as medics were doing the best they could. She wished she could have his resolve, but she also knew that deep down he was as scared as the rest of them. The tank commander looked up at her and instantly recognised her even over the distance. He gave a friendly and informal salute that she acknowledged. Silva carried on.

"Reiter's equipment has gone into production. I hear some units in the US have already been issued it. Whatever is needed, it must be done. We need that gear, and we need it now!"

Chandra turned to look at the flood of enemy swarming towards them and prayed for it all to be over. Let it all be a bad dream, she thought. It can't be real, none of it. She felt numb from the misery and loss she had witnessed. Then her attention was drawn by a cough and a splutter behind their trench. She turned to see Hall rolling in pain.

"He's alive," exclaimed Silva.

Chandra clambered out of her trench and rushed to the Corporal. He rolled over onto his back and looked up at her with a smile, even though she could see the pain in his face and blood pouring from his mouth. She knelt down beside him and looked for any wounds. His rifle lay splintered in half beside him, having taken the worst of the impact. She could see that his right shoulder was dislocated and slung low.

"I'm still here, Major, still in the fight," he smiled.

She lifted his other arm and looked for any wounds. He

winced in pain, but she was relieved to see his wounds did not extend further.

"You're a lucky bastard, Corporal. We'll get you patched up and back in no time," she replied.

He sighed in pain once again and spat blood out onto the dirt where his broken rifle lay.

"Major, we gotta sort this out. We're getting fucking killed out here. What happens when they get here in greater number?"

She heard footsteps as the mud squelched beside her and saw Sergeant Silva step up to her side.

"He's right. We haven't got the firepower to stop them at a distance, and at this range, we were god damn lucky no more got through. Two or three of those in the trench, and we could have all been done for."

"Alright, I hear you loud and clear. I'll do what I can. You get the Company back for re-supply."

"What are you gonna do?"

"Whatever I can to get us what we need."

* * *

Kelly strode through the corridor that was lined with eager troops waiting to re-take the ground they had been losing on a daily basis. What was left of the Moon government still did their utmost to stop him going into combat, but he would not be swayed. He could never ask his fellow citizens to fight while he watched from safety.

The Chinese transport has taken back their remaining children and wounded. Those left knew they were stuck there for the foreseeable future. It was a grim reality, but at least now they had hope. Kelly reached the intersection where Martinez and Chen were awaiting him. All three officers carried the M97 launchers with armour piercing rounds that had proven so effective in their last major battle, even if it was ultimately doomed to failure.

"I'm heading north to take the passages we lost last week," stated Kelly. He pulled out his Mappad with a layout of the passages. "Chen, you go north-west through 49B. Martinez, you'll follow me until you reach this intersection, at which time you'll take this section, corridor 38C."

"That'll have us crossing paths within hours. We could cover more ground than that if we work further afield," claimed Chen.

"In an ideal world, Colonel, but this isn't an ideal world, or at least not anymore. We underestimated the strength of their forces once, and I will not do it again. If we fail again, it could be the end of us all. I appreciate your troops are eager for action, but we know all too well the horrors that we face."

Chen nodded in agreement. Kelly could see the Colonel didn't agree with his assessment or tactics, but he was loyal enough not to contradict them.

"Your being here is greatly appreciated and will never

be forgotten, Colonel," said Kelly to reassure the Chinese officer.

"What is the estimate of remaining enemy forces?" asked Martinez.

"A hell of a lot left for Earth, so I can only imagine they have left what they believe is enough to keep us suppressed."

"That's reassuring," he snarled.

"What do you want me to say, that this is going to be easy? These Krycenaeans, or whatever they are called, didn't come here to take power. They came to take our lands, and they will not rest until we are dead. Remind your men of that. It's us, or them. The Earthers have opened up an opportunity for us, so let's not screw it up."

Kelly turned back to Chen who still looked less than enthusiastic about his plan. The Commander couldn't tell if it was their mission, or the fact the Colonel had to fight on the Moon which bothered him.

"The colony may mean nothing to you, Colonel, but that shouldn't matter. You have seen the pressure Earth forces have laid down that has opened up the gates for us. Know that in fighting here, you can do the same for them."

"Damn right, killing these freaks is killing these freaks, wherever you do it," Martinez mused.

Chen smiled.

"Actually, I'd rather not be fighting anywhere. Life as

a soldier used to be an adventure, and a safe one at that. Now look where we're at."

"And someday you can go back to that life, Colonel. Wars don't last forever."

"As long as you survive them," he replied.

Martinez turned around so he could see the Colonel with his only good eye.

"Hey, we've made it this far. Those bastards thought they'd run us into the ground, and we're still here, and still standing."

"And plenty aren't."

"You signed up to be a soldier, Colonel. That means you signed up to defend your nation and its people against any threat that may be posed against it. Do you think any soldier ever got to choose his opponent?"

Chen dipped his head in shame. He knew he was being selfish, but it was hard not to be when he was being asked to risk his life for a colony that had in his lifetime felt quite alien. He finally looked up and nodded in agreement. Kelly did not blame Chen for his lack of motivation in fighting for them or wanting to risk his life. The Commander no longer valued his own life. He had grown comfortable with the idea it had been given up for the greater good.

Kelly had lived an easy life as a military Commander of a colony that saw no action to speak of. He had spent much time reading of great battles and commanders of old. He had become well accustomed to what he must do, and the sacrifices he must make. He always admired those officers and leaders who had led from the front, even though it may lead to their deaths. He saw himself like the great Philip of Macedonia. But he also knew he would likely meet the same bloody end that so many great combat leaders did.

A small price to pay, he thought. Kelly's life had seen little excitement and noteworthy events. He didn't mind dying for a just cause, but he prayed his exploits would be remembered. Dying alone, and his accomplishments going unknown, was the only thing that scared him anymore. At least now he knew the children and other vulnerable citizens had been saved.

"This is the time we have been waiting for, and the time to strike back on our own terms and with a fair chance. It ain't gonna get any better than this. Good luck to both of you, and relay my regards and gratitude to your troops, any questions?"

The two men said nothing. Martinez had been numbed of the fear of facing the enemy guns, but Chen had seen little action since arriving. They had mostly spent the last few weeks hiding away from the devils on the surface.

"Alright, let's do this."

Kelly slung the launcher over his shoulder and quickly turned, walking away with a quick stride. Martinez followed close behind. As Kelly grew nearer to his troops, he could feel his stomach turn. He had given up hope of survival, but now that a new challenge grew nearer, he could feel concern flooding back into his mind. *What if we fail? What if I get them all killed? This could be the end of everything. We can't fail.*

The troops were parted either side of the broad corridors watching the two officers stride past. A few whistles rang out as they saw their leader approach the front line. It was one of the few morale boosting experiences they ever had in their miserable and seemingly hopeless lives. Martinez paced up further, so he could walk beside the Commander.

"Do you think we can do it? Do you really think we can do it this time?"

The Commander's voice had no concern, and it was calm and considered. He did not raise his voice loud enough for any of the passing troops to hear, nor was he trying to back out.

"Honestly, I think we have a chance, and the best we'll have."

"So you weren't bullshitting?" he asked.

Kelly shook his head side to side.

"If I thought there wasn't a reasonable chance of success, I would never risk the lives of us all."

"Really, you sure you don't just want to go out in a blaze of glory?"

"What use is that when there'll be no one left to know it happened?"

Martinez smiled. It was the first reassurance he had

gotten in weeks. Some might have thought Kelly was a selfish glory hound from such comments, but Martinez took it as a sign that he wanted to live. The two men reached the access doors to the next tunnels that no one had stepped foot through in weeks. The entrance had remained hidden to the Mechs who patrolled the nearby corridors. Kelly turned back to address the closest troops. Lieutenant Perera was at the head of them; a man who was no stranger to the death the enemy could deal out.

"For too long have we hidden in our caves! Every week the enemy breach a new corridor and discover new ways into our homes. Each week we lose more of our friends to such attacks. Eventually, we will run out of places to hide! The Earthers have given us a chance here, a chance to save ourselves. Let's grasp it with both hands, and kick these alien bastards out of our homes!"

The troops cheered, all but Perera. He was still doubtful, like so many of the officers, that another sally out could work. Few, but those in charge, knew of the death toll from previous actions. Kelly could see the doubt in the man's face, but he no longer had the time to convince every soldier that they had hope. He turned and grasped the huge wheel locking the door shut.

Martinez and the others watched in suspense as the Commander spun the lock around until the door opened just a millimetre. Kelly didn't show any caution. He knew he must be confident and forthright. With his weapon still slung across his back, he took the door wheel in both hands and hauled it open. The half-metre thick door creaked as it swung its hinges and rocked back against the wall.

Commander Kelly strutted confidently and triumphantly out into the dusty tunnel without a weapon in his hands. He turned back and looked at the troops who peered on in amazement. They were roused by his seemingly unflinching confidence. A cheer rang out as they rushed forward to join their fearless leader.

Kelly turned on the spot and lifted his weapon. He suddenly became aware that he no longer felt like the old and creaky desk worker close to retiring that he had done. A rationed diet and regular combat had conditioned him. He had shed kilos of weight in the last few months. Gone were his chubby cheeks, replaced by a sharp and grizzled jaw. His armour fitted right. His body felt right, and his troops could see the resolve in his eyes. It's our time, he thought.

"Let's take these bastards down!" he cried.

Gone was their calm concern and caution. They got to a jogging pace and rushed down the corridors. The stomping of hundreds of boots echoed down the empty cavities. Kelly turned a bend to find a single Mech stood gazing in awe of the noise and frozen in utter shock at what it saw. Before it could react, the Commander and five others lifted their weapons, releasing a hail of gunfire that killed the alien in seconds.

The troops cried in a bloodthirsty frenzy as they rushed past the body of the invader without even breaking stride. Gunfire erupted in the distance where Chen had made his entrance. Kelly smiled as he recognised the volley of human weapons.

"That's our lads!" he yelled.

They had cut down another four Mechs without any injury by the time they reached Martinez's designated corridor. He nodded in recognition to the Commander, lifting his rifle and leading his troops off at the fork. They had maintained a jogging pace through half a kilometre of tunnels and found only a few enemy guards.

"Is this really it? Are we finally taking it all back?" asked Perera.

Kelly turned to see the officer was at the front and by his side.

"This has gone on long enough, and it's our time," replied Kelly.

The Commander could see new life in the Lieutenant's eyes. The hope that had been lost so long ago had returned within minutes. It was all the motivation Kelly needed. He no longer felt tired and beleaguered. It was as if he had awoken a different man that day. They were no longer the hunted.

When they finally reached the rendezvous point, they could see the same rush of excitement amongst all that fought beside them.

"Status report!" shouted Kelly.

"Corridor is clear, one wounded," replied Martinez.

"Clear, one dead, two wounded," shouted Chen as he rushed towards them.

Kelly's smile grew wider. He never liked losing a single soul, but a single death after all the devastation they had witnessed was a better result than any of them could have hoped for. He spun around to see the faces of the troops around them. They were not panting, and they were not downtrodden. Smiles and excitement filled all their faces. Kelly knew that it was an opportunity he must take advantage of.

"Colonel Chen. You felt we may better clear this ground if we fought further afield. Are you still confident with that assessment?"

Kelly deliberately shouted it loud enough for all near them to hear.

"Yes, Sir!" Chen yelled back.

"I'm heading north, Martinez, east, and Chen, west. Let's clear these bastards out of our land!"

The troops thrust their rifles into the air and cried with excitement. Kelly could hear the applause ring out through the corridors around them. He could not relay his words to their armies, but they knew well enough that success was in their hands.

"Let's do this, forwards!" cried Kelly.

CHAPTER SEVEN

Chandra walked past lines of billets with a sombre tone. She walked without meaning or purpose. She knew they had just a few hours until the main enemy attack, and that there was little else to do.

"Major!"

She looked up to see Sergeant Silva approaching. She responded in a dull and lifeless manner as if she had lost all care in the world. She wondered why they were even bothering anymore. So many of her friends were now lost. Their own side seemed to be the cause of as many of the losses as the enemy. She had always told the Company how they were fighting for the human race, but she now felt like she was in foreign lands more than ever.

"What is it, Sergeant?"

"Captain Jones! He's been cleared for duty and will be reporting back to the Company within the hour!"

A glimmer of hope appeared in her eyes, but it was soured by the thoughts that rushed to the front of her mind.

"He's being returned to us now? He can't be ready for it. What, are they emptying all the hospitals or something?" she insisted.

The Sergeant looked taken aback by her response.

"This is Captain Jones we are talking about. You have wanted him back since Amiens, and we need him now more than ever."

"No, we need the Jones that we knew months ago. I am not sure that man exists anymore. Have you not seen him since his return?"

Silva shook his head. He had seen the horrors at the prison camp where they had rescued Jones, but he had assumed that the Captain would quickly recover.

"I think you have gravely underestimated the trauma that Charlie has been through. God knows I would have done anything to avoid it, and anything to have him back. Schulz is emptying the hospitals of any soldier who can hold a rifle, but he isn't ready to be back here."

"Sorry, Ma'am, but I'd rather have half the man the Captain used to be stood beside us, than not at all."

She glared into the eyes of the Sergeant. For a moment she was furious with him for talking back at her, but she took a deep breath and calmed herself. Silva had become a great friend to her, more than she could have imagined or her military discipline would approve. Officers and NCOs were always a world apart for her, as she had been taught. But times had changed, and Silva felt her equal more than ever, proving as such on a regular basis.

"Major, we need all the help we can get."

She nodded in agreement. She never saw what Silva and Taylor had on that frightful night of the rescue, but she had seen the Captain since and knew enough to be concerned.

"I can't put Jones back in any position of command, not until we know he is up to the task."

"Yes, Ma'am."

"Your platoon is without an officer. I will attach Jones to your unit, on the basis that you remain in command until I say otherwise. Jones will be in a liaison officer position only. I need him looked after, Sergeant."

"Understood."

"Charlie is one of the best men I have ever known, and one of the best officers, but God knows what the last few months have done to him. Whatever horrors we have faced, they are belittled by his. Keep a careful eye on him, and keep him safe. I don't fear for our own lives, but for his."

Out of the corner of her eye, the Major caught a glimpse of a familiar face, that of Legrant, the Mayor of Amiens.

"Excuse me, Sergeant."

BATTLE EARTH III

"Of course, I'll inform you as soon as the Captain arrives."

"Thank you, Sergeant."

She was vague as she strode off with meaning past the Sergeant. Silva turned for a moment to see what the cause of her interest was. He instantly recognised Legrant. He watched for just a moment and held his breath, as he realised what Chandra might be getting into. He turned and strode away. He knew that the last thing he should do was interfere and smiled as he walked away, in the knowledge that Legrant was perhaps going to get some of the punishment that he deserved.

"Bastard," Chandra muttered under her breath, and she rushed towards the French Mayor who had been the cause of Jones' capture and Walker's death. A look of dread overcame the man's face as he saw her a moment too late. She swung a hard hook into his face that knocked the man off his feet. Legrant landed hard on the concrete floor and was almost unconscious.

Two French policemen who were with the Mayor tried to draw their pistols but were not quick enough. She wrenched her pistol from her thigh and trained it on the Mayor's head.

"Don't even think about it!"

Silence overcame the area as soldiers all around turned to marvel at the sight. Chandra's uniform was heavily worn and covered in mud. Her face was filthy and dry blood still stained her jacket from the wound she'd received that very day. Despite it all, her rank was still visible and that alone stopped anyone from interfering. The two police officers stood frozen, not knowing what to do. They could see the crazy expression in her eyes and realised she was fully willing to kill them both where they stood.

Chandra finally looked down at the Mayor who was still flat on his back and wincing in pain. Blood trickled from his mouth, and the back of his head had landed hard on the ground. He wore a perfectly tailored suit and overcoat which was previously impeccable. She smiled in the knowledge that his coat would now be filthy and frayed.

"Do you remember me, you bastard?"

Legrant stopped writhing in pain and looked up at the barrel of the gun and then to the face of his attacker. He remembered her as his face went pale.

"I'm sorry, I had no idea..."

"No fucking idea?" she cried. "We were there to protect your town, and what did you do in return? A man died because of your stupidity. Another has been left as an emotional wreck after being left at the mercy of the enemy, and a further good man was killed while trying to rescue those who were captured because of you!"

Tears came to the man's face as he broke down.

"I had no idea... you have to believe me. I thought I was doing the best thing for my people."

"Why? Why!" she turned and paced up and down

before him in anger, not knowing what else to do. She noticed one of the cops reaching for his gun and quickly lifted her pistol. She fired off a shot that narrowly missed his arm and struck the wall behind the man. He flinched and froze in astonishment.

"What have you given in this war? What have you sacrificed? We have been out there from the day this war began, fighting and dying to save your lives. Captain Jones, who you detained and left to die, he had been fighting in the defence of France since it all began. What possessed you to do something so stupid... so wicked?"

Sergeant Silva appeared at the scene, having heard the gunshot. Two military policemen were close behind, but he held up his hand to stop them.

"Major, this isn't the way!" he yelled.

She spun around in shock to hear a friendly voice. It was almost enough to make her put the gun down, but then the memories flooded back into her mind.

"Do you know what this man did!" she cried.

Tears were coming from her eyes, and her cheeks were red. Silva had never seen Chandra in such an emotional state.

"I know. I was there, and I know exactly what he did. But that doesn't give you the right to be the judge, just as he had no right to do so with Jones."

She stumbled over the Mayor and knelt down beside him with the gun barrel resting on his chest.

"I could kill you, right now. I would if I could. Don't you know the pain and suffering you have brought?"

Legrant nodded in panic.

"I'm sorry, but I couldn't have known."

"You knew what you were doing was wrong! You detained friendly forces in a time of war. That is treason, and you should hang for it!"

"Major, this is not for us to decide," stated Silva.

"Why? He did!"

She broke down into tears but didn't let the gun go. She could handle the pressure of her job, but she could not understand the betrayal of her own people.

"What can I do? Anything?" whispered Legrant.

She looked up with fiery red eyes and a hateful expression.

"I don't want you to do anything. This isn't about me. Can't you understand that?"

The cop she had shot at spoke.

"Major... Chandra, is it?"

She peered up scornfully at the man.

"I am truly sorry for your loss. But you should know the reason for us being here."

She stayed silent and continued to glare at the man with utter disgust. She remembered the town's police and their role in it all. To her they were just as complicit as Legrant.

"We came here to volunteer...to fight."

"What?" she muttered.

"The Mayor, Legrant, has organised many police forces from the eastern French provinces. We have volunteered to fight under his command."

She looked down at the Mayor to study his response.

"Is this true?"

He nodded with sincerity.

"Why? Why would you do this now?" she asked.

He lifted his sleeves and whipped off his brown, sliding back so he could rest his aching back against the nearest wall. Chandra stayed on one knee with her pistol in one hand awaiting his response.

"I was wrong. I know that now, but you have to understand, I thought I had no choice. But I can see now that it was wrong, and I would do anything to make up for my mistakes."

"You can't bring soldiers back from the dead, and you can't remove weeks of horror from a man's mind."

"No, but neither will I put a gun to my head and pull the trigger, for what would it achieve? I came here to offer up everything I have to give. We will fight alongside you and die if that is our destiny."

Chandra lowered her gun and dropped her head into her left hand. Everyone watched and waited in anticipation. Nobody made a move against the Major. They already knew how quick her reactions were. Silva broke the silence.

"You are really doing this? You will fight beside us?" he asked.

Legrant nodded, and the other policeman spoke up.

"We know we have shamed ourselves, and that shame may never be taken away, but let us do something to help."

Chandra lifted herself up onto her feet and holstered her pistol. The MPs didn't move. They knew the reputation of the Immortals all too well. They also knew they couldn't afford to detain a key officer before the imminent fight. Silva breathed a sigh of relief as the situation was cooled. The Major strode up and stopped a few centimetres before the Mayor's face.

"I'll never forgive, and I'll never forget. God save you, if you lied about this. You have a debt to pay, and don't forget it."

She turned and strolled off towards the Sergeant. The MPs stood silently as she ignored them. They wanted to avoid trouble as much as Legrant did.

"You okay, Major?" asked Silva.

She strode past him without a word as she wiped the tears from her face.

"Fuck," he whispered as she left.

Silva knew that Legrant was the last thing they needed right now. Chandra was a tough officer, more so than any, but he knew it could be enough to finish her off. They needed a reason to keep fighting, and the French Mayor was a reminder of how little they were appreciated. He considered pursuing her, but he knew it would be a mistake.

BATTLE EARTH III

* * *

"Captain!" yelled Monty.

The two brothers rushed to their feet to greet the officer who they had all but lost hope in ever seeing again. He still looked gaunt compared to when they had last seen him and with a paler face. He smiled briefly as they rushed towards him.

"Welcome back!" shouted Blinker.

Jones nodded. It was good to be back with his unit, but he could already see that it was a shadow of its former self. Silva appeared in the doorway to their billets and stepped towards him with a smile.

"Good to have you back, Sir."

Jones ignored the three men as he peered around at the billets and saw far fewer familiar faces than he would have expected. Many of them enthusiastically got to their feet, but he continued to look confused.

"Where is Captain Friday?" he asked.

Silva shook his head with a woeful expression. Jones' face barely changed upon the news as if it no longer affected him.

"How?" he asked casually.

"On some bullshit mission we were sent out on."

"Some shit never changes."

Silva smiled, he was glad to see the Captain still had some sense of humour, despite his ordeal. He rushed forward and grabbed Jones in a strong bear hug and pulled him off his feet.

"Damn good to have you back, Sir!"

He planted the Captain back on his feet. Jones gasped to get air back into his lungs and smiled at the welcome he had gotten.

"Honestly, we've taken a beating, and we need all the help we can get right now."

Chandra appeared at the doorway and looked in with both curiosity and concern. Jones could see the worry in her face, and the sign of the recent tears she had shed.

"Reporting back for duty, Major!" he shouted.

Despite her concerns, Chandra was overcome with excitement at seeing her friend among them once again. She stepped cheerfully down to see him and shook his hand.

"Welcome back. I am sorry to say there will be no time for pleasantries. The Krycenaean armies are coming down the road from Saarbrucken with everything they've got. We've got little air support and still no access to Reitech equipment."

"So apart from that, all is good?" he jested.

Chandra smiled, and for a moment, she saw the old Jones before her once again. He was always a light in the dark, and a cheery face when all was miserable. She was reminded how much he meant to her and the Company. With Friday gone, and Taylor still detained, it was good to have him back.

"I'm attaching you temporarily to Silva's platoon, and he will remain in command. I hope you can understand the importance of maintaining the status quo this close to combat?"

Jones nodded in agreement, but she could see the disappointment in his face that after all he had been through, he was not getting his command back. There was little she could do about it.

"Got it, Major, I'm here to help wherever it's needed."

"You sure you're ready for this?" she asked.

"No place I'd rather be."

That's what concerns me, she thought.

"I've been away a long time, and I want some payback, so point me in their direction, and I'll give 'em hell."

Chandra turned to Silva.

"Form up the Company, Sergeant. We fall out in ten."

Before the Sergeant could bark his orders, a wing of enemy craft rushed overhead, strafing pulses of energy across the base. Jones did not even flinch as the others ducked for cover. Debris from a nearby building was thrown across the street and landed at their feet. Chandra turned to see Jones stood tall as if nothing had happened. She could already tell that he had lost his reason to live. He was still just a shell of the great man he used to be.

"They can't be far now," she said.

"2nd Inter-Allied! Form up! Form up!" cried Silva as he

brushed aside debris and got to his feet.

Thirty minutes later they lay in the trenches once again. They were at the back this time, owing to their part in the earlier battle. The lines of human defences were almost silent as they watched the enemy cover the last few kilometres. Friendly artillery roared in the distance and overhead but was far enough away it seemed like little more than background noise. They could see the forest before them flatten as the huge enemy tanks rolled through what they believed to be an impassable natural barrier.

Thunder rumbled in the distance as heavy rain clouds appeared to follow the enemy to their position and water began to pepper their helmets. The ferocious bombardment before them was causing some trees to catch alight, but the rain quickly extinguished them. The tanks behind their trenches opened fire when the enemy came into range. Their guns roared as they fired one volley after another.

The troops could see the forest being torn apart for kilometres in either direction, but they could still see the slimmer of movement and rustle of trees as the enemy continued to advance.

"How can they keep coming?" asked Blinker.

"They're like machines," replied Monty.

Chandra could already feel the fear that was rife in the ranks. Nobody expected to be able to hold what was coming for them.

"They aren't machines! They're creatures just like us. They can be killed, they can be broken, and they can be defeated!" she yelled.

The Company stayed silent, hearing other officers shout similar words of encourage in languages they couldn't understand. The trenches were five lines deep, spanning as far north and south as Chandra could see. But in all of their lines, the position they stood in seemed to be the focus of the enemy advance more than any other.

"We can't hold here," whispered Silva to Jones.

"Maybe not, but maybe it doesn't matter anymore," he replied.

Silva turned in shock to see the Captain's deadpan face. He could see that he no longer had any reason to live. He looked down at the oncoming enemy with a hatred he had never before seen in any man. Jones was the only one among them who was not afraid. He was not tense, and he was in his element. It was in this moment that Silva realised the Captain's purpose there. He wanted to go down fighting. He wanted to commit suicide in the only meaningful way he knew.

The Sergeant wanted to grab and Captain, there and then, and beat some sense into him, but he knew it was too late. The he began to wonder, Maybe Jones is right, and maybe there is no purpose to it all anymore. Jones turned to Silva and stared into his eyes.

"You promise me one thing, Sergeant."

"Anything..." he replied.

"Whatever happens here, you make certain Taylor isn't left in that cell to rot when the enemy rolls over the base? I don't care what you have to do, and I don't care who you have to kill. You get the Major out, you hear me?"

Silva thought about it for just a moment. The fear of death seeped away as he thought about the Major. For the first time in weeks, he thought himself thankful to be free. At least he could affect his destiny. Silva could see the fear and dread in Jones' eyes that another one of them would be left in the clutches of the enemy.

"You have my word, Captain. You have to know that we did everything we could to get you back."

"I am well aware of it, Sergeant, and never think I hold any of you guilty for what happened to me and Walker. That was beyond your doing. Now let's be sure it never happens again. You saw that camp, and you have some idea of what went on there. You be certain to put a gun to your own head before you ever have to face that. Better still, go down fighting."

Silva reached forward and slapped his hand down onto the Captain's shoulder.

"I'm not going anywhere, Sir, and neither are you. We're back together for the first time since Amiens. Together we are unstoppable."

"But we aren't together, Sergeant, not yet. Taylor is the back bone of this Company."

Silva gritted his teeth as the smile was removed from his face. He hated to think of the Major locked up just a few kilometres away. He turned as he heard the sound of crashing trees grow nearer.

"They're almost on us."

"And all we've got are these fucking peashooters," replied Jones.

Silva missed the liveliness that had inhabited Jones at even the bleakest of times. That light within him had been driven down deep inside and he knew it may never come out again.

"ARMALs at the ready! cried Chandra. You are free to fire at the four hundred metre mark!" she shouted.

"Did you really lose all your gear for rescuing me?" asked Jones.

Silva nodded.

"When Taylor found out you may be in Metz, he went to Schulz with a plan to get you out. The General expressly forbid him from going through with it. That night he did it anyway. The General's been making us pay ever since."

"Christ, all this for me, was it all worth it?"

Silva turned with a look of shock.

"Don't blame yourself for this. This is Schulz's doing, and someday he's going to know about it."

Chandra had heard half of their conversation and turned to look at Jones as he waited calmly with his rifle in his hands. He noticed her gaze and turned to return a smile. She saw there was some glimmer of the original man in his body, but it was deeply buried. Getting Jones back only made her remember how important it was that she secured the release of Taylor.

"Good to see old faces back, Major?" asked Parker.

"Bet your arse. Taylor's next, and don't you forget it."

"I'll hold you to that, Major."

They lowered themselves into their trenches as the enemy breached the final wall of the forest, and their tanks rolled across the barren and war torn plain. The energy pulses intensified as their positions were pounded by enemy fire. Their trench works protected them from most of the incoming fire, but the aerial attacks and artillery bombardments still tore trenches apart along the line.

After a long wait, the Major heard the troops of the first trenches open fire as the enemy came into range. It was only a minute later that the second trench opened fire. She crawled back up to the trench shelf to survey the scene and gasped as she saw hundreds of enemy vehicles and thousands of Mechs advancing towards them.

"My, God!"

She felt her lips were dry, and her throat was sore. Her breathing stopped for a moment as she realised that they couldn't hold. Parker crawled up beside her and had much the same reaction.

"What the fuck are we going to do?" she asked.

Chandra shook her head in astonishment, but she had

no answer. Explosions erupted along the lines of the enemy as the artillery bombardments continued, but they continued to pour from the forest in a seemingly never-ending column.

"Prepare to fire!" she cried.

The first of the enemy forces were now less than a kilometre from their trench and in range of their rifles, but not of their effective penetration. Campbell had already opened fire with his high-power rifle, but it was doing little to scratch the numbers pouring towards them. The Mechs and vehicles were already laying down fire on the move, and the trenches were getting ripped apart.

Mines erupted as the enemy passed, and thick black smoke poured into the sky, but it did nothing to hinder the enemy advance. Chandra wondered if they felt anything at all. Are they heartless? Are they truly nothing like us? she asked herself.

"Fire at will!"

The Company opened fire, joining in with the other units. Tracers rushed across the battlefield as many of the creatures were stopped in their tracks by the sheer quantity of ammunition striking them, but few were falling.

"Bastards won't die!" yelled Yorath.

"How can we stop them with this shit?" muttered Suarez as he continued to fire.

They watched as many of the creatures took close to a hundred rounds to eventually stop. The first lines of

Mechs were cut down as they closed to three hundred metres, but it was not enough. Hundreds more of the metal clad enemies filled their places, and drones continued on between them.

Chandra watched in horror as a dozen of the Mechs reached the first trenches and leapt in like fanatics, thrashing around and firing as they crushed all before them.

"Grenades and ARMALs into that trench, now!" she yelled.

Several of the Company looked at her with pity when they realised they were being asked to fire on friendly forces.

"There's nothing more we can do for them, fire now!"

Light pulses continued to flash in the first trench, and they raised their weapons and readied themselves to fire. Screams of agony and pain rang out as they threw a dozen grenades and fired off ARMAL launchers forward into their own positions while the soldiers ran for their lives. Seconds later, the ground shook and earth from the trench blasted into the sky, and all within it were silenced.

The bodies of Mechs and humans together were scattered either side of the crater for all to see. Silva looked to Chandra with a bleak and defeated look.

"We can't do this!" he shouted.

She looked around to see the first line of trenches had been overcome in several places along the defences. Her mouth was open, and her eyes wide at the horror she was seeing. We can't hold. We're fucked, she thought.

"Major!" shouted Parker. "We have to get the hell out of here!"

"Run? Who is going to keep up the fight? Who is going to stop them?"

"There's nothing more we can do here!"

She looked over to see Captain Jones stood on top of the trench, screaming insults at the enemy and firing as quickly as he could downhill into their positions. Pulses erupted all around him. He wants to die, she thought. It was the final confirmation she needed that their time was over.

"Fall back, everyone fall back!"

Silva turned in relief, and he relayed the orders with his booming voice along the lines. As he did so, he noticed Jones still stood up above the trench, reloading his rifle with no concern for his life. He reached forward, grabbed his ankle and pulled. Jones was thrown off his feet and landed hard on his back. Silva grabbed his webbing and hauled him back into the trench. An explosion erupted where the Captain had stood just seconds before.

The two men were thrown back against the opposite wall of the trench and showered in dirt as they were deafened. Silva stumbled back up to try and regain his senses but was grabbed by Jones.

"What the hell are you doing? That was my time. My

time to die! You have no right!"

Silva shook his head from side to side and coughed, trying to regain his senses and make some sense of what Jones was yelling about. He slapped the Captain who stumbled back and stood over him with anger.

"You may not give a shit about your life, but the rest of us do! You are needed here, so get your fucking act together, and start acting like a soldier!"

"Retreat! Retreat!" shouted Chandra.

Silva grabbed Jones, tossed him out the back of the trench and leapt after him. He hauled the Captain to his feet, pulling him along as they rushed back into Ramstein. Chandra looked back to see the survivors of the trenches clambering out and retreating in a frenzy. The armour that was at their backs was already beating a retreat and firing to give them cover.

"Where are we going, Major?" shouted Parker.

"Just follow me!"

The Company reached the first buildings of Ramstein, and enemy fire continued to pound the complex. They knew the tank traps and trenches would slow their advance for a while, but they had little time to escape. They'd been jogging for five minutes when Silva finally rushed up beside the Major. Until then, nobody cared where they were going, providing it was away from the enemy.

"What's the plan, Major?" he asked.

"The plan is you follow my lead!"

It wasn't long before they arrived at the military prison that only Chandra had ever seen. The others quickly realised their purpose for being there. Strong metal doors protected the entrance. She stopped them at the door and looked back to Blinker.

"Give me that ARMAL, Private!"

"With pleasure!" he replied with a mischievous grin.

"Major, you sure about this?" asked Suarez.

"More sure than anything in my life!"

She lifted the weapon up onto her shoulder and fired without hesitation. The doors of the building were blown off their hinges, and dust sprayed out over the already filthy troops. She threw down the device and lifted her rifle from her side. Chandra rushed forward into the dust cloud and with a dozen others at her back.

Silva was the first in behind Chandra, with Jones following quickly behind. They stepped through just in time to see the Major's rifle stock strike one of the MPs and knock him to the ground. She flipped the weapon around and shouldered it with the sights trained on another sat at a desk.

"Major Taylor, release him now!"

"You know I can't do that."

She quickly fired two rounds over the man's head, one of which clipped his cap and tore it off his head. The MP froze in utter shock.

"You heard the lady!" shouted Silva.

"Uhh... yeah... okay, but you'll never get away with this."

"Get real, son, have you seen the shit that's coming our way?" asked Silva.

"Fuck this," muttered Jones.

He turned and rushed through the prison. Seconds later two shots rang out.

"Go after him!" shouted Silva.

She rushed off down the corridor after the Captain.

"Don't you know what's going on out there? All hell's coming down on us. You need to release any prisoners you have, and get the hell out of here!"

"Release them? We have strict orders!"

"To hell with your orders, do you know what the enemy do to any survivors?"

The man shook his head in surprise.

"Well I do, so unlock the fucking cages now!"

The man stuttered and reached for the keys as Silva gave him some encouragement with the barrel of his rifle. Jones appeared at the edge of Taylor's cell where the Major was laid flat out on his bed. He got up with a look of utter shock and amazement.

"Jones, you're back?"

"Damn straight."

"You busting me out?" he asked.

"Bet your arse, you didn't think we'd let Schulz keep you locked up forever, did you?"

Chandra rushed into view, as Jones shot the lock off

the door of the cell and heaved it back. She was greeted by a broad and cheeky smile across Taylor's face.

"You're in this, as well? You know what Schulz will do to you for this?"

"None of it matters, anymore. Ramstein is overrun, and we have to get the hell out of here!" she shouted.

"Run, where?" he asked in surprise.

"I'll tell you on the way. Let's go!"

They rushed past as the guard passed them in the corridor, fumbling with his keys.

"You know I've done some serious shit in my time, but this? We ever get caught, and we're goners?"

"If we'd left you any longer, you'd be dead anyway," replied Jones.

They rushed out of the building to find armoured trucks rolling up. Taylor half expected it to be Schulz coming to arrest them all, but they were greeted by Sergeant Dubois.

"How on earth did you find us?" asked Chandra.

"You don't think I knew this would be the first place you'd be when all hell broke loose?" she asked.

"You got space?"

"Climb in!"

The Company rushed to fill the vehicles and climb on top. Explosions erupted all around the base. Their anti-aircraft defences continued to pour fire into the oncoming craft, but they were only able to destroy a handful of their attackers. Pulses smashed down into the ground as the five vehicles rumbled forwards and out towards the western entrance. They watched in despair as the base was hit by barrages; so heavy that many of the buildings were flattened.

"I thought you'd never come. All that time in that cell, all I could think about was all of you, fighting where I should be," murmured Taylor.

"Schulz has been a thorn in our side all the way. Maybe now we can get free of his idiotic grasp," replied Chandra.

He turned to Jones with a smile.

"And you, you made it? Back in uniform, and at the front of it all again."

Chandra smiled, but thought back to the suicidal scene she had seen at the trenches. She couldn't bring herself to discuss it so soon after finally getting Taylor back, but she knew it was a new obstacle to overcome. Despite the fact that they were yet again on the run, she couldn't help but be thankful to have Taylor back among them.

"We lose anyone?" she asked Silva.

"I saw one of Suarez's platoon killed and a few from mine wounded, but we got off pretty lightly," he replied.

"What will we do now that Ramstein has fallen?" he asked.

The others listened in intently.

"General Schulz may be a bastard, but he isn't an idiot. All forces that have arrived in the last couple of months have been establishing a tiered defence over the next twenty kilometres east. We always knew a push like this was possible, and that we couldn't rely on a single barrier to stop them."

"Christ, he really has done his homework," replied Taylor.

"As I said, a bastard, not an idiot. I have no doubt the Generals will have been the first out before the base fell, and they will be eager to know how you escaped."

"What will you tell them?"

"The truth. You've seen what the enemy does to human prisoners. It was my duty of care to ensure your safety. Quite frankly, I believe the General will have enough on his plate to worry about you right now. He needs every soldier he can get, so he'll just have to put up with you."

"You really thought this through, hey, Major?" he jested.

"No, I'm making it up as I go along, and it's just working out for the best."

Taylor smiled, and he knew she wasn't joking, although it still didn't sit well with him that the circumstances of his rescue were attributable to the deaths of probably thousands of soldiers. He got up and stepped up towards the driver's seat where Dubois was at the controls.

"You saved our asses again, Sergeant, you our guardian angel or something?"

She smiled as she looked back, gazing at Captain Jones. Taylor smiled, noting her affection for the Captain. He looked back and could see the blank expression on Jones' face he remembered from when rescuing him. He could see that Jones was not the man he used to know. His heart sank, knowing that it was all for nothing.

200

CHAPTER EIGHT

Taylor sat in a cold damp trench once again. He still wore his prison issue white clothing, and the light of day hurt his eyes. Of all the places to be in life, he would never have wanted to be where he was in those circumstances. And yet after his incarceration, he was revelling in his freedom. He lay back against the soggy earth that stained his shirt and took in the fresh air. They were a couple of kilometres from the main line.

"Major!" He looked up to see Silva drop a clean set of BDUs into his lap. He recognised the camouflage pattern as used by the Germans. It was a darker and more disrupted pattern to their own, but it had been fitted with his rank insignia and American flag."

"Best I can do."

Taylor sat up and looked at the hand-stitched insignia and smiled.

"Much appreciated, Sergeant."

He stood up and pulled off his damp and dirty clothing where he stood and pulled on what Silva had brought him. It was comforting to once again be wearing proper attire, even if it was improvised. He peered around at the troops around him and noticed that a handful of others in their Company wore the same.

"It's pretty hard to get replacement gear from the States, right now. I guess the postal service is slacking," Silva grinned.

The troops looked a hotchpotch mix with three uniforms being prevalent amongst them now, and most were heavily worn and faded. He looked out east across the open plain. He could see line after line of trenches as far as the eye could see; with tanks dug in to hull down positions, and serviceable turrets from destroyed vehicles setup as emplacements.

"Looks like the troops here have been busy."

"We had no idea. We thought when Ramstein fell we were in the shit. Turns out everyone expected that to happen. I guess it ain't surprising, considering we lost Paris and all that."

Taylor suddenly realised he'd fallen into a daydream while lying down and peering up at the sky. A couple of hours had passed, but it had done him some good. He'd got better sleep out there on the edge of a muddy trench than he'd ever had in prison.

"Chandra and Jones about?"

"They've been called up to Command."

"Ah, shit, Schulz know I'm out?"

"No idea, but he doesn't miss much."

"Ain't that the god damn truth?"

A new round of shelling rang out in the distance. They were too far from the action to see it, but they all knew the kind of relentless brutality that was being thrashed against their defences. Taylor looked out over the forest canopy to the west to see plumes of smoke rising and alien craft on the skyline.

"Poor bastards."

"Hey, we've done more than our fair share," replied Silva.

"True, but I wouldn't wish it on anyone. To have to live through such a time... what did we do to deserve it?"

"Wrong place, wrong time, I guess."

Taylor chuckled. He admired the fact that Silva could never be reduced to the depression and misery that plagued so many of their fellow soldiers in such dire times.

"Do you know what our orders are?" asked Taylor.

Silva looked up with a bemused expression. He'd never in his life heard the Major ask him such.

"I don't believe we even have any. Allied forces have been ordered to dig in all over, but I doubt anyone even knows where we are, right now."

"How did Chandra get called up then?"

"Despatch riders relayed the command."

"Then I guess they know where we are!"

"I wouldn't take it for granted, Sir. Communication and organisation has gone to shit. As far as I know, the only stand is to dig in and hold your ground wherever you are."

"That worked a treat in Ramstein."

Silva sighed, as he knew it to be true. Taylor hadn't been at the front line, but he knew all too well what it was like to face their invaders with such antiquated equipment.

"I hear the first production Reitech gear has been issued," stated Silva.

"That scuttlebutt, Sergeant, or have you seen it with your own eyes?"

Silva shrugged his shoulders as Taylor looked at the horizon lighting up in the distance with artillery fire. Facing the Krycenaeans was a fearful thing, but he hated knowing that fellow soldiers were dying just a few kilometres away while he stood and chatted. He turned back to Silva.

"This tiered defence. It'll work you know. Or at least, it has the best chance of working, but it'll cost countless lives."

"Which option wouldn't?" he retorted.

An hour later, Chandra returned hitching a ride on a Jeep along with Jones. They found Taylor sat with a mug of coffee staring aimlessly out towards the raging battlefield.

"Good to see you back in proper gear!" she shouted.

He turned and leapt to his feet.

"What are our orders? Am I to be arrested again?"

"Schulz knows you're with us, but he doesn't know the circumstances of how. There's not much he can do about it, right now. He can't spare the people, or time to sort you out, and doesn't even have anywhere to keep you. His orders are that you are to remain under my custody and may carry a weapon, but have no privilege of rank until a full investigation and tribunal is possible."

"Jesus, what a fucking asshole!"

"Give the man some credit. He's letting you walk free, and that's all that matters, right now. For the foreseeable future, you will remain as my consulting officer."

Taylor shook his head in astonishment.

"I guess it's better than prison."

"Look, as far as the Company is concerned, you're still a Major, and they will take your orders, no matter what. As long as you stick with me, and we maintain that capacity publicly, you'll be fine."

"Alright, and my weapons?"

"Gear is still tight. We are to beg, borrow and steal whatever we can get. I believe Suarez has a spare rifle, and that will have to do."

"A rifle, you've seen what those creatures can do? We barely survived when we faced them the first time with gear like this!"

"All I can say is be thankful we are alive, and not at the front," she said as she gestured towards the front lines which Taylor had been so fixated on.

"They'll get to us eventually," replied Taylor.

"I have no doubt, but that time is not now. Let's get some rest while we can. We have rations being brought up within the hour."

She stepped forward and strode past the trench onto the next where the other platoons were set up. Taylor quickly rushed to her side and paced along with her.

"There's word Reitech gear's being issued, you know anything about that?"

"Only the same rumours you do," she snapped back.

The two of them turned as they heard vehicles roaring towards them. Two trucks were racing over the mottled ground away from the front lines. They could already make out a dozen or more wounded on each of them.

"Christ, they're getting murdered out there," Chandra said.

"Tiered fighting, there'll be a lot more before it's over. This is a war of attrition now."

"Aren't all wars?" she replied.

Chandra strode away, leaving Taylor watching the trucks of wounded pass by. It was a demoralising sight for the rest of the troops to have to witness. They could make out the blank and lifeless expressions of many of the casualties. Others screamed in agony as medics worked on them deeper inside the vehicles.

The troops of the 2nd Inter-Allied watched for two days as the wounded were ferried back from the front, and the artillery and bombardments drew nearer. They could tell the enemy was now just two kilometres away, and so they waited anxiously each day to see if they would have to fight. They could only hope the losses on the enemy side were as significant.

"Giving ground every hour doesn't seem like the best move," mused Campbell.

"It's a solid tactic. It may seem like we are giving up ground and losing a lot for it, but you lose troops however you fight. Think about it, you set up one big wall, and if there is one breach in that wall, you are finished. Spread your forces in deeper layers, and each breach by the enemy is less significant. They get further and further away from their resources and can never bring everything to bear against one target."

"And the troops at those front tiers? Are they expendable?"

"In a way, yes, but soldiers fight, and soldiers die. Sacrifices have to be made."

"Not always wisely, though. It wasn't so long ago you said Schulz had no care for the soldiers in his command, has that changed?"

"Probably not, he is a bastard, but that doesn't make

him wrong."

Taylor could hear a few vehicles heading towards them from the east. They had gotten used to seeing trucks transporting troops forward and casualties back, but he stood up beside the trench to look out. He didn't recognise the trucks. They weren't military issue.

"What the hell is this?" he asked.

Three trucks rolled towards their position. They were similar in size and layout to a regular army truck but of distinctly civilian usage. Chandra walked up to him and watched out of curiosity as they drew up to a halt. They half expected to be asked directions for somewhere, but could not understand why. It was a peculiar thing to see such shiny civilian vehicles in their warzone. The driver of the first leaned out and shouted.

"Major Taylor here?"

"You're speaking to him."

The passenger door on the other side of the truck opened, and they heard someone jump out. Seconds later, the passenger strode into view, and they were relieved to see it was Doctor Reiter.

"Major, I am glad to see you are no longer behind bars."

"Yeah, thanks for reminding me of it," jested Taylor.

"I hear the brass have been keeping you busy?" asked Chandra.

"Most certainly, Major, but I am sorry to see that you are no longer reaping the benefits of my work. I was sad to hear of the removal of the equipment from your Company and protested most vehemently on the subject."

"We've been fighting an uphill battle since. Your equipment gave us a fighting chance, but we've lost some good people these last weeks."

"Then you'll be glad to know that I am here to rectify that. I am returning all of the Reitech equipment which was issued you."

"Shit, are you serious?" asked Taylor. "Has General Schulz authorised this?"

Reiter shook his head and smiled.

"The General may decide what equipment he issues from the factory, but what equipment I build for myself and my testing, is to do with as I please. Your people remain the best test bed for my creations."

"We're getting it all back? Everything we had from you?" asked Chandra in amazement.

Reiter nodded. Taylor turned back to the trenches.

"Form up, and collect your gear!" he yelled.

A cheer rang out down the line as the troops hopped out of their trenches with an enthusiasm none of them had seen in a long time, not since before Taylor's arrest. Reiter gave a hand signal that was answered with a number of his assistants opening up the sides of the vehicles and hauling box loads of equipment to the edge of their trucks. The Company, who were desperate to get their hands on the gear, mobbed them.

"I can't thank you enough. Your timing couldn't be better."

"Yes, I can see," mused Reiter as he saw explosions erupt in the distance. "Now, last time we spoke you aired a concern about close quarter combat, and your lack of effective equipment at such ranges."

"Yeah, when those Mechs get close, they tear our guys apart," replied Chandra.

"Well, the return of your suits will go a long way to improving your strength and torso protection. However, I have a number of devices I believe will suit your needs. Follow me."

The quirky scientist led the two officers to the last truck, signalling for two of his assistants to lower boxes from the side with the robotic lifter. He flicked the catches and threw open the lid.

"The shield technology, you got it working?" asked Chandra.

"The targeting issue, yes," he replied

He lifted out a pair of protective glasses that appeared little more than shooting glasses, but with tiny power cells added.

"With this targeting device, you can aim and track your weapon independently, and in doing so, allow you to use it singlehandedly, providing you have the power of the exosuit to support the weight, of course. This will enable the use of the shield, as I predicted, to stand up to a number of pulse impacts."

"Outstanding," replied Taylor.

"Lastly, this little gem."

Reiter pulled out an implement that was almost a metre long and resembled a Roman Gladius, more than anything else.

"You wanted the ability to fight in close combat when such occasions arise. This is essentially a cutting torch with its own power pack. It'll charge off your suit when sheathed in the sheath designed for it."

Reiter handed it to Taylor, who looked at the odd looking device with a puzzled expression.

"This will really work?" he asked doubtfully.

Reiter looked up to his assistants and gestured for them to lower the next piece; a chest plate from a Mech's armour.

"I am calling this device the assegai, after the fearsome Zulu short fighting spear. When the device is drawn from the sheath, and grasped by the hand, it is active. If it is sheathed, or released from your grip, it immediately powers down."

Reiter nodded for Taylor to pull the weapon from its sheath. It weighed almost ten kilos and was a clumsy object without the power of the exoskeleton suits. He drew the assegai from its sheath, and the tubular blade was glowing and emanating enough heat for his chin to feel rather warm. Reiter pointed for him to test the weapon on the plate of armour that had been lowered down beside the truck. He turned to Chandra and looked at her with a puzzled expression.

"Go on, try it," pressed Reiter.

Taylor took a few steps up to the armour and pushed the assegai forward with force. To his surprise, he met almost no resistance and was taken off balance as the blade drove through the armour and up to its hilt.

"Christ," cried Taylor.

"I don't doubt that the assegai will be most effective at such ranges, but better it be you than me that has to do as such," claimed Reiter.

"You've done a damn fine job here. Does General Schulz know of this new gear?"

"I have told him that it is being tested..."

"Not by whom, I assume?"

Reiter smiled in response to the question she already knew the answer.

"Lastly."

"Not more? How do you find the time for all of this?" she asked.

"My dear, Major, few of my ideas are new. They are pet projects I have toyed with my entire life, or borrowed from by gone ages."

"What else have you got?"

"These flying enemy soldiers, I hear about. You most probably know that man-portable jet packs are not a new idea. No, no, in fact they have existed for hundreds of years. However, they always faced one major flaw, the age-old problem of power and fuel to weight ratio. Any device with enough power and fuel to be useful was too large and bulky. Anything compact enough, could only allow minimal flight."

"Go on," replied Chandra.

I have added on a booster pack to all of the suits I have returned to you. In addition to the aerial decent thrusters that you have used previously, you will now be able to make jumps of approximately a kilometre. The suit will have enough power for perhaps two or three of these."

"You mean we can fly?" asked Chandra in shock.

"Precisely, but only for those short periods, and you will need cooling off for up to ten minutes."

"And if we run out of power?" asked Taylor.

"Anymore than two jumps before charging the suit, which would require cable charging or a day in sunlight, and the suit will be a dead weight."

"You mean it'll stop completely?"

"Precisely."

"Shit, that's something to remember," Taylor muttered.

"Anyone else got these exo suits and guns yet?" asked Chandra.

General White has issued the first sets to Ranger and Delta units, I believe, as well as a select number of marines and others. They should be seeing use about now."

"Good to know, finally kicking some ass on the home front," replied Taylor.

"Now you must excuse me. This fighting stuff isn't for me, and I have plenty more work to do."

Chandra looked up at the eccentric scientist with a smile. She was fully aware he had gone above and beyond the call of duty to assist them.

"We won't forget this."

Reiter turned back one last time before he climbed onto the truck.

"Just keep doing what you're doing, all of you, and good luck!"

The two officers turned and looked in amazement at the masses of equipment left for them, and that the troops were already eagerly rooting through. Chandra turned to Taylor.

"This big push through Ramstein, if they'd been able to do it weeks ago, they would have."

"You're thinking they've thrown in everything they've got?" asked Taylor.

"Yep, one big push to try and break our armies. If you can stop them here, we may just pull victory out of the hat."

"It's a tall order," he replied.

"Tell me a single stage in this war that's been simple? This enemy underestimated us. They underestimated our ability to adapt and overcome. I believe they are starting to see the possibility for failure."

"Then let's make sure they do."

* * *

The fighting had raged on in the distance and gradually closed on the troops of the 2nd Inter-Allied. They had watched as the wounded poured back towards peaceful lands. For once they were eagerly awaiting their foes. Taylor looked down and admired the new equipment he wore. He knew in his head it weighed more than he could ever manage, but it felt less of a burden than the gear he'd become so accustomed to in the corps.

"You know if it wasn't for Reiter, we'd probably be dying here?" asked Chandra.

Taylor nodded at the grim realisation that hadn't struck his mind.

"Let's not fear for what could have been. We're here now, and ready to make those bastards pay."

"You know back in Ramstein, Jones was sent back to us the day we broke you out?"

"What of it?"

"He should never have been cleared for duty. You should have seen him out at the trenches. He wanted to die. He stood up in plain view of their fire and wanted to die."

"And yet he's still here?" replied Taylor.

"Not of his own accord. Silva dragged him from danger."

Taylor sighed. He had not seen Jones since that frightful experience at the prison. But it was enough for him to understand that no man could go through what he had and come out the same. It was the horror of being left behind he had so feared and been saved from. Morbid curiosity made him wonder all the time what terrors Jones experienced at the hands of the enemy. But every time Taylor thought of it, his stomach churned at the idea of being stuck in the situation himself.

"What do you suggest we do?" he asked.

"I didn't say I had an answer. You just needed to know."

"I am not sure any of us will come out of this sane, but he's alive and with us. Surely that's enough, right now?"

"Enough for what? Enough that he keeps pulling the trigger and knocking the Mechs down? Jones is worth more than that to all of us, you know that?"

Jones turned to Chandra with a scornful look.

"How dare you question that? I gave up everything for Charlie..."

Taylor's voice faded off as he looked around, checking none of the others could hear their discussion. Before he could continue, an explosion erupted just a few metres away. The two officers cowered down in their trench as they were showered in mud and clay. They looked up to see the remnants of the forward units retreating back towards them under fire.

"This has got to stop. Those alien scum don't get past this trench, do you hear me?" yelled Chandra.

Taylor looked around to see everyone's concern. The retreat did not help their spirits, but they were strong in the face of it all. As the retreating troops reached their trenches, Chandra stood up tall on the edge and called to them.

"Rally on us! Rally and fight with the Immortals!"

The hundreds of fleeing troops were mostly Polish and Czech forces. They looked in surprise at the Major's heavy loadout of equipment. They had all heard of the Immortals and their daring victories. Many slowed and began to listen.

"Fight with us! Join us, and end this fight!" she cried.

Troops of the 2nd Inter-Allied stood up in their trenches and followed their Major's example, beckoning for the incoming soldiers to join them. Energy pulses continued to smash the ground, encouraging the Inter-Allied to pick up their pace. Chandra could make out the silhouettes of the Mechs advancing and hissed at the sight of them.

"Come on, into the trenches!"

Pulses from the enemy armour erupted amongst them, instantly killing a dozen as they desperately retreated across the open ground. She hated Schulz for putting them out there to die, but she still understood the necessity for doing so.

The fleeing troops slid into the trenches and landed hard among the Company. A Polish Sergeant rolled in beside Chandra and landed hard, almost breaking his neck. She reached forward and hauled him to his feet. Being without the Reitech suits for so long had made her forget what strength it gave. The man looked up at her in fear as his arm was nearly wrenched from its socket, and he flew into the trench wall beside her.

"Sorry about that, Sergeant!"

"No problem, Sergeant Jankowski at your service," the man replied cheerfully as he winced in pain.

He ducked back down as further pulses smashed around them.

"They're coming in fucking hard, Major. You honestly think you can stop them?" he asked.

She turned to see allied armour rolling down the roads to assist them. She looked north and south and could see lines of infantry dug in and in desperate need of a morale boost. Finally, she turned back to the Sergeant.

"We've done enough retreating for one day. It's time to give them a taste of their own blood!"

The Pole smiled, but she could still see the doubt in his eyes.

"Be ready for 'em!" she yelled.

Taylor looked down at the huge rifle he held in one hand and admired it. It felt damn good to be back in the line. As much as he was grateful to be free, the rest of them were relieved to finally have back the equipment they had become so attached to.

"Eight hundred metres, wait for it!" Chandra ordered.

Taylor felt his finger close around the trigger in anticipation. As Chandra shouted out her last command, the roar of the tanks at their backs overwhelmed her voice, but it didn't matter. They all knew what time it was. The Company opened fire with everything it had, and the other troops who had joined them assisted. The gunfire rang out at such a rate it sounded like a constant drone.

In the first volley, Taylor saw fifty Mechs killed instantly and riddled with fire. The Poles and Czechs watched in astonishment and cheered. They knew their weapons had little to do with the destruction, but they continued firing anyway. They were caught up in the excitement of seeing so many of the enemy fall before them.

Energy pulses still rushed overhead and hit their positions, but the enemy couldn't put out the rate of fire of the allied troops, who were overwhelming them with the help of Reiter's equipment. They all watched in amazement as their armoured foes dropped like flies at three hundred metres, and their tanks could do little better.

As the incoming fire began to calm, Chandra stood up to look far along the line. She could see the trenches on their flanks only just holding while they were making mince meat of the Krycenaeans. She took a pace further up, out of the firing shelf and out onto the open plane, where she stood for all to see. She did not flinch nor kneel. Many of the allies stood and waited for her to speak.

"Let's finish these bastards now, and drive them back from where they came!"

She turned and leapt across the open trench work; jogging towards the oncoming enemy with her shield held out in front and continuing to fire as she drove forward. The Company watched as two pulses smashed into her shield and barely slowed her. They were still doubtful of the new equipment, but Chandra was all the proof they needed. Taylor leapt out of the trench after her.

"Kill them all!" he shouted.

The Company launched out of the defences, and the other troops soon followed. They were inspired by the officer's valour and unfaltering courage. The Company rushed forwards with their shields close together, providing plenty of cover for the other allies behind them. For the first time in weeks, Chandra could see doubt in the Mechs. She couldn't see their faces, but their body language spoke volumes.

The creatures were turning and looking for support, but they weren't finding any. As the Company advanced, they took shots at the enemies on their flanks which drew attention from the other trenches. The allied soldiers for a kilometre either side watched with open mouths as they rushed forward towards their enemy.

The thought of closing against the Mechs was frightening, and something to be avoided at all costs. General Schulz watched from a hilltop three kilometres away through a digital viewing screen. He was speechless as he saw them rush across open terrain.

Taylor and the others quickly realised they could fire with a fair accuracy even at high speed, thanks to Reiter's tracking devices. They were closing the distance fast with the enemy who were being whittled down at quite a rate. Taylor rushed forward to get to close quarters first. The Mech he charged fired at close range, jolting his shield arm with the impact. The burning light almost blinded him, and he felt it singe the hair on his arm underneath his gear.

Firing as he ran, the Major hit the Mech with two shots square in the chest, but he didn't slow down. He lifted his shield and smashed it into the creature at an almost sprinting speed. Much to his surprise, he smashed the huge beast onto its back as if they were football players. He lowered his rifle and fired a further two rounds into its faceplate, and thick blue blood gushed out from the holes.

Chandra fired on full auto as she rushed towards a Mech, and knew she had killed her target before it had even hit the ground. But as she turned to find another target, a broad door on a burning tank she was passing flew open and smashed into her shield. The impact launched her into the air, and she tumbled several times in the mud.

She landed nimbly on to her knees and looked up to see

a creature half climbing out of the hatch. Before it could get its second foot from the opening, Captain Jones thrust his assegai up into its stomach region, driving it high into its torso. Blood seeped down the weapon and over Jones' hand, and he stood marvelling at his work.

Jones drew out the blade and watched the beast tumble lifelessly out of the vehicle down into the mud. He looked over to Chandra who looked in disgust at the gory sight.

"They really do work," he stated.

The Major was glad they had the assegai devices, but she doubted it was necessary in that moment to use them. Jones is fuelling a blood lust, she thought. Nobody chooses to fight these creatures in close quarters unless they have no other choice. It was further confirmation that Jones was on the suicidal path she had predicted, but there was no time to be concerned with it in that moment.

Chandra turned to see that Taylor had climbed up onto the wreck of a Mech vehicle and was using it as a vantage point to pick and choose his targets at their flank; and so assist their troops to the north. She turned around to see the allied armour at their backs had advanced and were already spreading out to assist.

"We've done it!" shouted Monty.

"We've fucking broken through the bastards!" cried Blinker.

Cheers rang out across the trench works either side of their positions, and they could see the Mech forces already turning to face them. Chandra knew their breach would allow them to roll up the enemy flank, a fact she was all too eager to exploit. The allied tanks turned sharply to head north to help. She turned to the south and screamed.

"Forwards!"

She raised her weapon towards their enemies, screaming with all the power of her lungs. Taylor's face lit up in a frenzy as he leapt from the ruined vehicle. They fired on the move as they had done before. Only two of their Company fell, one wounded and one killed. Taylor rushed to the flank of an advancing enemy tank and drew out his assegai. He thrust it into the side door mechanism and cut through the lock like butter.

Chandra watched as Taylor sheathed the assegai and ripped the door from its hinges while it continued forward. He lifted his rifle and put the barrel through the opening, firing into the compartment with a bloodthirsty grin on his face and his teeth clenched. She could tell he was enjoying dealing out death; she was only glad he had vented his anger on the enemy and not their Generals.

Two hours later, they stood at the heart of a burning battlefield. The bodies of allied soldiers littered the fields; only outnumbered by the debris and wreckage of the Krycenaean forces that had been mauled on the open plain. Chandra eventually found Taylor once again. The marine Major had enemy blood trickling down his face and staining his uniform.

She knew that Jones was not the same man she used to know, but neither was Taylor. Jones had a death wish, but Taylor was hungry for blood. He smiled as he panted and scooped in the stale air. Cries of excitement continued down the allied lines. The only words they could make out were 'Immortals!' being screamed en mass.

"We've done it, broken the cycle," said Chandra.

"You think that'll be enough for the brass?" asked Taylor.

"Well, we didn't exactly stick to the plan, but fuck 'em. No one can doubt what we have achieved here today."

"Why should it stop? We've got them on the run, so let's keep moving forward and finish them!"

Chandra stepped up closer to the Major and whispered.

"All in good time, let's savour what we have and re-group."

Taylor's wide eyes settled as he calmed himself. He knew she was right and was starting to see the brutal and bloodthirsty hunger within him that he didn't like. He hunched his shoulders down in shame and looked away from Chandra. She grabbed him, stopping him from walking away.

"Hey! You've done a great job here today, and don't let anyone tell you otherwise. If Schulz wants to bitch about it, then tough shit!"

Taylor smiled, but it wasn't his concern at all. Confinement had made him a little crazy, and he could already see in himself a part of the emptiness he'd witnessed in Jones. He ridiculed himself in his mind for comparing his hardship with that of the Captain. He sat down on top of the torso of a fallen Mech. Gunfire continued to rage all around as the rest of the human armies drove the Mechs back. He watched in amazement as he could see the creatures in the distance turn tail and flee.

Captain Jones strolled up to the Major with his weapon slung on his back and not a care in the world. Blood still stained his clothes and skin. He looked out at the enemy with a frenzied look. Taylor felt like he should have a witty comment for Jones, but he knew it would be lost on the dire Captain. Chandra rushed back to them.

"Come on! What are you stopping for! Let's drive these bastards back to hell!"

Jones wrenched his rifle from his back and eagerly stepped forward at the idea of further bloodshed. Taylor yawned as he stood up and wished for it all to be over. He turned to see Parker. He'd barely spoken a word to her since his rescue. Her face was filthy, but her teeth shone through with a dreamy smile. It was a vivid reminder of what he was fighting for.

"Come on, Major, we've got work to do," she whispered.

He turned back and watched as Chandra and Jones led the Company into the flank of the enemy, firing as they ran. His fatigue suddenly seeped away as he got his second wind and leapt into action. For all the fear and dread the enemy caused, they were now being slaughtered in a turkey shoot like none of them had ever seen.

An hour later, they stood on the bloody plain with the enemy utterly vanquished. Taylor looked out towards the tree line and could see the rest of their forces had halted at the sight of the destruction. Chandra felt a warmth in her stomach that their foes were being made to suffer as they had. Now they can know what it is like to live in fear, she thought.

CHAPTER NINE

Taylor sat once again upon the battlefield surrounded by the dead of both sides Have we broken them? Soldiers passed him with smiles and patted each other on the back for a job well done. He felt a new kind of hope, like he'd not felt since the beginning. It was a hope so long forgotten that it felt entirely alien to him.

A column of vehicles approached from the east and he could already make out stars on the bonnet of one of the armoured cars. General Schulz coming to claim his victory, thought Taylor. Chandra paced up to him with a smile which quickly turned to scorn when she saw the incoming vehicles.

"Ahh shit," she exclaimed.

"Yep, no peace," he replied.

"You're gonna have to take this lightly. Schulz has let you off the hook, but he will be quick to anger, so no macho bullshit, okay?"

"That an order?"

"You're damn right it is. The last thing we need is to lose valuable members of this Company over some stupid pissing contest."

"Yeah, yeah, I got you."

Taylor watched nonchalantly as the impeccably clean vehicles rumbled into view, and General Schulz jumped triumphantly onto the battlefield. He spun around with a huge smile as he looked at the success they had won, and reached out to shake the hands of all the soldiers he passed. He stepped up towards Chandra and quickly noticed Taylor sat down beside her. At first his face turned to scorn, and he tried to ignore the American Major, but he knew it would be in vain.

"Major Chandra, what is this new equipment I see?"

"Doctor Reiter wished to field test new equipment, and we did it for him."

"Fascinating."

He turned to look down at Taylor and knew he must do something to smoothen over their hatred of each other. Chandra's Company was invaluable to him, and Taylor was an important part of that."

"Major Taylor, I see that you and this war are inseparable."

Taylor looked up at the General with a tired and uninterested expression.

"That seems to be my curse."

"You must understand that I never wanted to have to punish and detain you, but neither can I have my army running amok. The chain of command must be adhered to."

Taylor nodded, as he had nothing left to say. He'd never stop hating the General for his spineless response to the captured soldiers, and his subsequent incarceration for doing the right thing.

"Damn good work here, Major Chandra. Get some rest. The first issue of Reitech equipment is going operational this evening. Tomorrow we push on into France!"

He waited for an enthusiastic response from the Major, but it never came. The thought of returning to the lands where they had been so badly mauled did not appeal one bit.

"We'll be ready, Sir."

"I am sure you will," he said with a smile.

The General turned back and shouted out words of praise to the troops as he returned to his vehicle, to be spirited away to the life of comforts he rarely left. Taylor lay with his head in his hands. His return to the Company hadn't been all that he'd envisaged. Friday was gone, and Jones seemed to be a different man altogether. Boots squelched in the mud, and he saw Parker looking down on him. Her smile was enough to make him forget it all. They had one night to spend together before the fighting continued.

* * *

"Major, Major!" shouted Blinker, rushing along the lines of popup tents where they had spent the night. Chandra stood beside a kettle awaiting her coffee while Taylor sat down next to her cleaning his rifle. She turned casually to see what the fuss was about, but showed little enthusiasm. The rain hadn't let up overnight, and it was a soggy and bleak start to the day. The Private rushed up to Chandra and didn't wait for her to answer before continuing.

"Major, the order has been sent out. We're going forward across the border!"

She didn't even look at the Private as he spouted out the news with such enthusiasm. She'd no stomach for returning to France; the land only conjured up memories of pain and suffering. The Major slowly stood up and stretched her legs, taking a sip from her mug as the Private watched in surprise at her lack of response.

"We're going back, Major, taking back what we lost!"

She nodded slowly in response and finally replied.

"Relay the orders to Sergeant Silva, and have him form up the Company in fifteen."

The Private turned to Taylor to look for any spark of joy at finally being on the winning side, but he found none. He sighed and rushed off to relay the orders in some hope of a response more pleasing. Chandra turned to Taylor who was waiting for her to speak.

"They have driven us back this far, you really think they're going to give up France this easily?" she asked.

"Not a chance. I think we have hit them hard, and more than they could ever have expected. But to underestimate this enemy now would be a grave mistake. We stopped them before, at Paris, and Ramstein. Maybe this time is different, but it sure doesn't feel like it yet."

Within the hour, they were geared up and moving forwards across the war-torn lands still littered with the bodies of their enemies. They paced cautiously towards the forest edge where just the day before they had seen the enemy forces amassing. It was suspiciously quiet, but an hour later they had passed well into the undergrowth and found no sign of the Krycenaeans.

"You really think they are on the run?" whispered Parker.

"We've certainly bloodied their noses a little, who knows?" replied Taylor.

"Well that's reassuring," she snapped.

It wasn't long before they reached the far side of the forest, and once again looked on at the Ramstein base. It seemed abandoned and peaceful. Chandra lifted her hand to stop the Company, beckoning for Taylor to come forward to her side.

"You think they'd leave a strategic point like this for us

to just walk back and take?" she asked.

"No fucking way. No, I wouldn't."

"That's what I thought."

The two of them lifted their binoculars out and zoomed in to look at the positions ahead of them. Taylor was drawn to a small flicker of movement and a reflection as the sunrays bounced from a metal plate, but it was soon gone again.

"You see that?" he asked.

"Yeah, nothing human could have survived there."

"It came from one of the eastern trenches."

"Shit, you think they're digging in?"

Taylor carefully studied the terrain once again.

"Would make sense. I think we've presented a tougher challenge than they thought possible. We starting to knock the bastards down in open ground, and it would only be logical for them to dig in."

Chandra sighed.

"As much as it is good to know they are feeling the pressure, them digging in is the last thing we need."

"Yeah, gonna be a real bitch."

She turned to Silva.

"Sergeant, get me a line to HQ."

Silva relayed the commands down the line. They still had to carry wired spindles as they advanced in order to remain in communication. They were a cumbersome and difficult means of contact, but they were already starting to get used to it. Before the radio had reached Chandra, she heard tank tracks rolling to the north. She turned to see a tank regiment advancing quickly in column towards the base without any regard for what may be within.

"God damn it, get me that radio now!"

"Fools, they're gonna get themselves killed."

Blinker rushed forward to the Major's position with the portable radio and wires trailing behind him. She ripped the handset from the box and yelled her warning to the operator at the other end of the line, but it was already too late. A volley of light lashed out in the distance and tore through the first two tanks, destroying them instantly. They watched helplessly as the column spread out and tried to engage the enemy to little avail.

Half a dozen vehicles were reduced to burning hulks, and the others beat a hasty retreat. Taylor could see through his binoculars that they had little to show for their losses.

"God damn, they're dug in hard!"

"Just like we were," replied Chandra.

A call came down the handset for the Major.

"We've got enemy entrenched along the eastern perimeter of Ramstein, requesting immediate artillery support, over."

"Roger that, fire support en route. Hold position until further notice, over."

The Company lay quietly amongst the scrub just forward of the forest they had so recently departed. The foul lung-filling smoke from the friendly vehicles was quickly reaching them. They all could smell burning flesh in the thick smoke, and it was enough to make them want to vomit.

"We're in for the long haul," whispered Chandra.

The light on the field phone flashed, signalling an incoming call. She ripped the handset up to here ear.

"Major Chandra here."

"Major, your company is ordered to dig in. You will have the appropriate equipment within the hour. Until that time, stay put."

She signed in relief. As much as she didn't like sitting around with nothing to do, facing the entrenched enemy was a frightening proposition. She found a fallen tree and sat down on it without a care in the world. She was confident they were out of the enemy's range, but to the rest of the troops it looked like a defiant statement.

"Dig in? I thought this was our big push?" yelled Taylor.

"We can't run onto their guns," she replied.

Taylor sighed and spat into the mud beside them.

"After all this, we're being stopped by our own tactics?"

"Adapt to the enemy, isn't that what we have been doing?"

Taylor strutted back and forth with frustration until he stopped at the sight of Jones. The Captain stood out in front of them all. He stood tall and also without a care in the world. He was fixated by the glimmer of enemy movement in the trenches far off into the distance. It was as if he longed to engage them in battle. Mitch turned back to Chandra, who had noticed the Captain but chosen to ignore it.

"He isn't right... Jones," stated Taylor.

Chandra ignored the comment and stared ahead.

"He isn't the same man we used to know. I am not even sure he should be in combat."

She finally turned and looked with scorn at Taylor.

"I'd have Jones beside us if he was just half the man he used to be. None of us are the people we used to be, and never will be again," she whispered.

Thirty minutes later their trench diggers arrived, and as the sun faded on the horizon, they sat quietly on the firing shelves. They had quickly become accustomed to long waits and cold wet nights spent below ground. Taylor and Chandra sat either side of the base of their trench with their rifles propped up and out of the way. They both knew they were far from any combat.

"Is there no way this war can end without the total destruction of one side?" asked Chandra.

"I don't believe so. We have seen the evil inside those creatures and their disregard for life. I...I have looked into their eyes and tried to reason."

Taylor went silent.

"Karadag... you told me about him after Poitiers. You saw him again, didn't you?"

Taylor looked at her with a fiery hatred and fear in his eyes.

"How did he survive the nuke?" she asked.

Taylor shook his head in disbelief.

"I just don't know, but I pray none of us have to face him again."

Taylor couldn't speak anymore of the enemy leader. He had filled his thoughts since the night he was nearly beaten to death by the sadistic alien. He wanted payback, but the thought of encountering the beast again made him doubt he would survive the experience. He looked up to see Parker sitting on the ledge of the trench a few metres away.

He had given little thought to Eli over the course of the recent fighting. All his attentions had fallen on the war that faced them. Their relationship appeared to rapidly be returning to that of Officer and NCO, which it always had been, although she still looked at him with a yearning when he wasn't aware of being watched.

The last of the light faded away, and the temperatures quickly plummeted. The exoskeleton suits regulated their temperature and kept them comfortable through the night. They could only imagine the freezing conditions the other troops had to endure. They had long been well equipped with the most advanced of cold weather equipment, but they knew it was high unlikely that any of it had reached the front line.

"I bet Schulz is sitting comfortably in the warm with his feet up," snarled Taylor.

Chandra smiled at Mitch's condemnation of their superior. She knew he had every right to be bitter. As they began to finally enjoy the peacefulness of the night, the sky erupted with a flash of light that was quickly followed by the far off thundering of artillery. Shells whistled overhead towards Ramstein.

The two officers leapt to their feet to look over the trench shelf and watch as the shells smashed into the enemy positions. They were too far to see what effect it was having, but they could make out the trenches bursting into flames. None of the troops cheered or jumped for joy, they were too numbed from the previous action. They thought of the brutal pounding they had taken from the enemy guns in the last months and wondered how much good it would do.

At midnight, the guns went silent to let the troops get what little rest they could, and deserved. Taylor sat cleaning his sidearm. Despite the little light they had, he knew it so intimately, he only looked at what he was doing out of the cathartic experience it gave. He could hear footsteps approach and snapped out of the daze he was in and quickly reached towards his rifle out of instinct.

Taylor paused as he recognised Eli and had a welcoming smile on his face. He felt his muscles relax and pulse slow as he moved his rifle aside to make space for her to sit with him. She relaxed down beside his shoulder so that he could feel her warmth, even through their clothing. It was a vivid reminder of the fun times they had shared back before the war.

For a moment, she didn't say a word as he reassembled the weapon. In the dead of night each component put back in place was audible through the trench. Parker watched his hands move with such precision and disciplined muscle memory. She was fixated on it until he finally locked the slide shut and holstered it on his side. He turned to Eli and gazed at her smile.

Mitch lifted his arm and wrapped it around her. She rested her head down on his shoulder. He knew it couldn't be comfortable resting on the straps of his body armour, but he appreciated the sentiment. Taylor looked up at the stars. It was a luxury that had been long forgotten, and the cloud cover the previous day had given him little opportunity to enjoy the night sky.

Chandra watched as Taylor and Parker fell asleep against each other in the trench, looking at them with a warm heart. It pleased her that in the middle of such bloodshed and near apocalyptic disaster, there was still time and room for love. She thought back to Friday, and the spark of feelings she had begun to feel for him; and the sorrow his death had brought.

For two days the Company held put in the tree line. They were well supplied, but it was a painstaking waiting game. The artillery roared throughout most of the daylight hours, and the infantry sat uneasily awaiting combat. They watched as the base, they'd recently known as home, was flattened by their own forces.

On the morning of the third day, Chandra awoke to Blinker tapping her on the shoulder with the field phone in his hand. She rubbed her eyes as she yawned and took it from him. Taylor woke and stood up, waiting to hear their orders. She listened carefully for a few moments and put the phone down, looking up with a sigh.

"It's time. We're going over the top."

Taylor smiled at her reference to the First World War. The fact they were only a few kilometres away from the bloody battlegrounds was a vicious reminder of how brutal a war could be. Taylor remembered documentaries which had calculated death tolls in their tens and hundreds of thousands, but it was never something he could ever fully comprehend. Now those horrendous numbers had meaning to him. Every single digit of those vast numbers now meant something to Mitch. He realised that each one was someone like himself, Eli, Chandra and the rest.

"Form up! Form up!" she yelled.

The Company hadn't removed their equipment since setting up in the trenches, and their bodies were sore and creaky. They began to stretch and groan as they readied themselves to begin the assault.

"When do we advance?" asked Taylor.

Before Chandra could respond, they heard German techno music pulsate from huge speakers fitted on tanks concealed within the forest. Their engines roared to life, and the vehicles instantly lurched forward towards the battered ruins of Ramstein. The raucous music made the troops' ears vibrate, and it was a brutal way to begin the morning, but it certainly got their pulses racing and their blood boiling.

Chandra leapt up out of her trench and down on the edge, looking down on the troops. They stood silently waiting her orders; as the music made them angrier and blood hungry. She could see that other infantry companies on their flanks were readying themselves, and she could make out Reitech suits scattered throughout.

"For once, we go forward together! We lost France after a bitter fight, but this is the only ground the enemy has taken in Germany. For you marines, Ramstein is US soil, so would you let them keep it? We have turned the tide of this war, and it's now our job to seize this opportunity and drive them back to the sea!"

She got no response from the troops, but she knew they were each readying themselves for combat in their own way, and her words were coaching them along. A loud whistle blew out to the north, shortly followed by infantry clambering out of their trenches and continuing on after the advancing armour.

The first enemy artillery rounds were already striking

the open plain, and Chandra watched. She turned to the Company and lifted her rifle into the air.

"Let's give those bastards hell!"

They cheered as they leapt from their trenches and took to a quick jogging pace. Up on their feet, and closing the ground fast, they could begin to see the devastation their guns had rained down. There was barely a wall still standing in the eastern half of the former US Air Force base.

Light pulses surged towards them from the entrenched Mechs, but in lesser number than they had expected. Motor rounds from the advancing tanks continued to pound the Mech positions and limit their fire as much as possible, until they got within eight hundred metres of the positions. Chandra quickened to catch up with the armour, and as she closed within a kilometre of the trenches, she activated her jump pack.

"Jump!" she screamed.

The Major felt her stomach queasy as she was launched into the air at an immense speed. The others leapt into the air after her. As she reached the apex point above the enemy, she rained down fire on full auto until she quickly began her descent. Fear overcame her, as she descended at high speed towards the enemy and wasn't sure if she would slow down. She didn't know what she feared more, crashing to the ground or landing among the enemy.

"Shit!" she screamed.

As she thundered down to earth, her boosters kicked in and rapidly slowed her descent. She targeted the nearest Mech that was lifting its cannon towards her, and fired three rounds down into its head and shoulders. She had no control left of her landing point, crashing down onto the body of the creature as it was still keeling over and disappearing into the trench.

Taylor landed a split second after Chandra and sunk into the mud a few metres from her. He gasped to get his breath back from the death-defying leap, and saw the enemy turned their guns on him. Before he could fire his first round, the rest of the Company dropped in all round and opened fire down into the trenches.

Chandra clambered out of the trench and got to her feet. She could see Taylor and the others blazing away from the tops of the trenches, in what was more of an execution than a fight. Only two-dozen Mechs had survived the artillery barrage in their sector and were completely overwhelmed by their airborne assault.

Taylor looked around to see that their Company had already gone silent. The other infantry companies were nearing the enemy positions and taking heavy fire as they rushed across the open terrain.

"Major!" he shouted.

She turned to see him pointing south where a vicious volley of fire from the Mechs was mowing down allied troops. Mitch didn't wait for her orders. He took to his feet and rushed along the enemy lines to attack their flank; and was immediately joined by the rest of the Company. Chandra knew they were as loyal to him as they were to her, but she never let it bother her. She chased after the troops.

A number of the Mechs to the south could see the Inter-Allied Company rushing flank and turned to fight them. Taylor opened fire, charging with his shield held out before him. He reached the trenches, kept firing, and rushed past the burning body of the first creature and continued along their line. Some of the beasts he didn't even have time to stop and fire upon, but he knew his comrades were at his back.

Fire ripped through the trenches as the Company fired into the backs of the Mechs. Taylor reached a broad dugout at the end of the trench lines where three Mechs stood in position, firing at the incoming allies. He came to a quick halt and opened fire on full auto. He watched with joy as the creatures spasmed when the rounds penetrated their armour, and they finally tumbled into the mud.

The Major turned to see the other Mech forces had been utterly overwhelmed by their superior numbers and blitz attack. It was scarcely believable for any of them that they had finally led a successful attack against the invaders. For the first time since the war began, they were taking ground. Cheers erupted across the trenches and soon expanded to the others as the several kilometre-long perimeter of the base was claimed.

"You did this!" Taylor shouted to Chandra. "You broke their line!"

"No, Major, we did, together," she replied.

A second wave of allied troops reached them ten minutes later. They were astonished to see the work had already been done. They advanced on and took up positions in the ruins of the base, leaving the troops of Inter-Allied to rest among their vanquished enemy. Chandra walked through the troops, thanking them for their efforts.

"We should carry on to Paris!" shouted Blinker.

"Yeah, why stop here?" yelled Monty.

Chandra smiled at their enthusiasm.

"Ma'am, why not, there's no stopping us!"

She hesitated, knowing she must address the issue even though it could douse their high spirits.

"I like your thinking, I really do. But let us not forget how we have been caught out before. We have won a valuable victory here today, but let's not stick our heads up to get them chopped off. You just keep doing what you're doing, both of you. Get us a line to HQ, if you would."

When she had finally made her way around them all to praise their efforts, she strode back up to Taylor who was looking down at the lifeless bodies of the creatures. Chandra could already see some of the emptiness in Taylor's eyes that had overcome Jones. She opened her mouth to speak some words of comfort, but was interrupted by Blinker.

"Ma'am!" he cried.

The Private rushed towards her from the field they had just come from. The cable trailed behind him with the spindle in one hand.

"General Schulz for you, Ma'am."

She snatched the handset from his hands.

"Chandra here."

"Major, congratulations, and well done. Please convey my thanks to your troops, and Major Taylor in particular."

Chandra turned to Mitch with a wicked smile. Schulz is realising he must live with Taylor, no matter what, she thought.

"You must excuse me, Major. There is work to be done, and a lot is changing."

Her ears pricked up at the General's passing comments, but he was gone before she could pry any further. A matter of minutes later, shouts rang out across the line and cheers rang out. She could see in the distance that word was being passed along the line; causing the kind of excitement she hadn't seen in months. Soldiers rushed back and forth as the news spread. Suddenly, Yorath appeared in such a frenzy that he could barely contain himself.

"They're coming!" he yelled.

"Who? Who is coming?"

"Field Marshall Copley, and the whole bloody British army! They've crossed the channel!"

"What? Are you certain?"

"Yeah, British forces north of here are pushing forward to try and bridge the gap!"

She looked north and could see a huge dust cloud that was unmistakably the sign of an army on the move.

"Bloody hell, they've finally done it!"

She looked around to see the troops leaping in excitement. She spun back around to Blinker.

"Get a line to command. We need orders!" she yelled.

She looked to see some new life in Taylor's eyes.

"About time your people did some of the work," he jested.

An hour later, they were on the move to secure the rest of Ramstein but met little resistance. By nightfall, they once again occupied the trenches which just days before they had fled from under a brutal barrage and assault from the unrelenting enemy. They knew that the next day they would be pushing forward to the enemy stronghold of Saarbrucken, but for that night they could rest in the knowledge they had struck a vicious blow to the enemy. Chandra and Taylor sat once again in a trench as they had done the previous night.

"If they pulled out of Ramstein, they must be readying their defences for our advance. It'll be a hard fight gaining the next ground. They have over stretched themselves, but once they organise properly, we'll be up to our eyeballs in shit," said Taylor.

"Can't beat a bit of positivity," she replied.

"We did well today, but let's not forget what lies ahead."

"We'll take it as it comes, as we have done everything else. With any luck, we'll see some reinforcements before long, and get us back to battalion strength."

"I wouldn't hold out your hopes."

They slept uneasily as they each dreamt of the road ahead. When morning came, they awaited their orders to once again move forward; but thirty minutes after sunrise came, they heard booming engines high in the sky. The thick cloud cover of the dreary morning hid the source of the sound, and they all knew it was not human.

Chandra and Taylor watched the skies for several minutes until huge vessels broke through the clouds and roared northeast. They counted nine ships, and each looked as large as the Navy's most powerful carriers. The vessels were so vast that it was barely conceivable they were able to fly.

"My god, where are they heading?" asked Chandra.

"That's the way to Berlin, and they're opening another front right behind our armies," replied Taylor.

"How, I thought everything they had was right here, so where are these forces coming from?"

"I have seen them before, when we first encountered this enemy."

"The Moon?"

Taylor nodded. Though there was little fear or concern

in his eyes.

"You think they are feeling the pressure we are putting on them here? Enough that they'd send in everything they had?" she asked.

"I'd bet good money on it. They underestimated the human resolve and ability to adapt and overcome. I think they expected a much easier time of it on this planet."

"Still, this is going to cause us more than a few problems. We can't keep moving forward while they threaten us to the east."

As the droning engines faded into the distance, their attention was drawn to a jeep tearing along the craggy road towards them from the east. Only the driver was aboard, and there were no weapons or supplies visible. The two officers stood and waited for the vehicle. They both knew that its driver must certainly be coming to find one of them. A few minutes later, it skidded into view as the wheels locked, and it glided across the slick mud. The driver shouted out from behind the wheel.

"General Schulz requests both of your presence, immediately!" he yelled.

"You here to give us a lift?" asked Chandra.

"Sure thing, the General was quite adamant about the urgency of the matter."

She turned and paced back to where the Company was awaiting the advance west which was clearly on hold. The re-taking of Ramstein with minimal casualties had done a lot to boost morale, and she could tell they were eager to push forward but now knew it would not happen.

"Captain Jones!" she shouted.

The Major couldn't identify him among the troops until she could make out the outline of his back facing her. He had the look of a man that had lost all will to continue, but she refused to repeat the call she knew he had heard. He finally turned and got to his feet slowly and wearily. His face was bitter and cold. It was not a hatred of the enemy he expressed, but a lack of care for life.

"Captain, you're in charge until we return!"

Jones didn't even acknowledge her words, but she knew he had heard as well as the rest of the troops nearby. Sergeant Silva leapt to her side for a quiet word as she turned to leave. It was clear he shared some of her concerns.

"Major, are you sure Captain Jones is fit for this?" he whispered.

Taylor overhead the comments and interrupted her before she could reply.

"Jones is one of the finest soldiers I have ever known. He'll handle it."

Chandra sighed. It was an uncomfortable position she was being put in.

"There's no doubt that Charlie should have been given more time to recover before returning to his duties, but we cannot afford such luxuries these days. We need every capable soldier we can get. He's still the same man, after all. Remember that."

"Ma'am, with all due respect, I am not sure he is," replied Silva.

She stopped and turned back to look at the Captain who she had come to know as such a good friend. Perhaps he isn't the same man we used to know, she thought. Reluctantly, she nodded in agreement that Silva might be talking some hard truths.

"Captain Jones is the ranking officer while we are away, but keep an eye on him. If he shows any signs of being unfit for duty, then as a platoon leader, you have a responsibility to the wellbeing of these troops. You must do what is best for the Company. I pray that day never comes. Let's not forget the horrors the Captain has been through. He has been deceived and abandoned by allies before, so let's not allow him lose all hope."

A few moments later, the two Majors were aboard the jeep and on their way east to Headquarters. They passed over the crater-ridden muddy battlefield that had seen days of bombardment and fighting. Mech bodies still littered the terrain. The human dead were recovered periodically, but nobody had the care nor will to treat their fallen enemies with any respect. The occasional pyre burned in the distance where troops had gathered some bodies together in an attempt to cleanse the area.

Chandra and Taylor stood awaiting the General as he poured over maps and enemy locations. He finally looked up at the two but with a pale face. They could both see the fear in his eyes. The war was not going the way he wanted it to.

"Major Chandra, please come forward," he called.

She paced up to the General's table with Taylor close behind. Schulz scowled at Mitch, but he ignored the look.

"Major Taylor, let us set aside any reservations we have towards each other. We need all the help we have got, and we are on a tight schedule."

Mitch nodded in agreement. He still hated Schulz and blamed him for much of their hardships in the previous few months, but he also knew there was little to be done about it.

"I am here to fight as always, Sir," he replied.

Schulz begrudgingly accepted the Major's words while he knew full well that he was stubbornly refusing to accept any wrongdoing.

"You surely must have seen new enemy forces enter our atmosphere. They've recently put down just west of Berlin, and we predict that fighting will be underway within the next few hours. You know how thinly we are spread. What you achieved yesterday was impressive, and I thank you both for it. But this presents a great problem for us."

"Not enough troops to fight on another front?" asked Chandra.

"Precisely. The armies of Earth are fighting all over, and few as hard and often as yourselves. Berlin is lightly defended and to provide assistance would mean weakening our presence here. Splitting our forces could lead to the utter destruction of our armies here in Germany."

"What are you thinking?" asked Taylor.

General Dupont strode into the room and came to a sudden halt as he glared at Mitch.

"What the hell is he doing here?" demanded Dupont.

Schulz turned quickly and snapped at the Frenchman.

"We need the Major for this."

"We can't trust him anymore!" insisted Dupont.

"That's enough!" yelled Schulz. "Whilst I remain in charge of the armies here, I will decide who and how we use our resources. Major Taylor has more experience in fighting this enemy than any man alive."

Mitch smiled. He was amused by the obvious way Dupont was being disciplined by Schulz, a man who hated him almost as much as Dupont himself. Dupont was silenced, and Chandra turned back to the others.

"The truth is I am not convinced we can gain success on this continent, considering this new threat. It is true that Field Marshall Copley's army has moved into the north of France, but their progress is slow at best. With an enemy army at the gates of Berlin, we risk being divided and destroyed."

"So what have you got in mind?" asked Taylor.

"Your attack on the enemy weapon depot in Poitiers caused quite a stir. There is no doubt that it slowed the enemy massively and sent them into disarray, but a situation we were simply unable to exploit at that time. Our intelligence and surveillance suggest that it was not the destruction of the facility that had such an effect, but the harm done to their leader, who goes by the name of Karadag. Your mission reports state that you have already met this creature?"

Taylor's mind shot back to the brutal beating he took at the hands of the enemy Commander. It was not an experience he was ever inclined to repeat.

"Our reports show that this leader survived the nuclear device."

Schulz looked curiously to see that Taylor was not at all surprised by the information.

"You knew this? How?" he asked.

"I saw him in the Metz prison, during our rescue mission."

"And you never thought to report this vital information?" spat Dupont.

Taylor turned slowly and looked with utter despair and hatred towards the Frenchman.

"It was a little difficult to assist in this war from a prison cell," fumed Taylor.

"Gentlemen, that is enough! What has gone before us must be set aside. There may come a time when we must all answer for our actions, but now there are bigger issues at stake," interrupted Schulz.

Taylor took a deep breath to calm him, and the room went silent. Finally, Chandra spoke up.

"You think this Karadag is essential to the enemy? That they will fold without him?" she asked.

Schulz nodded in agreement.

"He barely survived the nuclear weapon, and several reports we have from the area show medical and recovery teams locating his badly wounded body. He'd lost a lot of blood by the time he was found. His recovery directly co-insides with the enemy advance through Ramstein."

"And you believe killing him could bring an end to it all?" asked Taylor.

"It's a theory, and one which all evidence would point too. I believe, as do many others, that the loss of Karadag could break their armies. They could lose the will to fight. We have to make them believe that this war is not worth the price, and not worth the sacrifices they would have to make."

"And if we kill their Commander, and it only makes them more blood hungry? They could well have someone more than capable of filling his shoes."

"I believe it is a chance worth taking. Our experts think it may work. I cannot order you to carry out this mission.

I would not will it on any soldier. But I firmly believe it could change the course of this war overnight."

Taylor looked to Chandra to judge her response to the news. He could understand why it was being asked of them and that it had a fair chance of success. He turned back to the General.

"Sir, please just answer one thing for me, honestly. Tell me you believe in this mission, that we have some chance of survival, and that the outcome could be as game-changing as you believe? Tell me you are not sacrificing our unit to make me suffer."

He could see the anger building in Dupont, but Schulz was a more calculating man. His strict leadership had led to much conflict between the two, but he could see Schulz was never dishonest. He was not the malicious and sadistic bastard that Dupont was.

"I promise you, Major, that I have every faith in this mission and your ability to conduct it."

Taylor thought for just a few seconds as he rolled around the ideas in the back of his mind.

"Alright, tell me the plan."

CHAPTER TEN

Chandra stood before every man and woman of the Inter-Allied Company in a briefing room that they could barely fill half the space. There were less than one hundred of them remaining. They had lost more friends than they wanted to remember. They were now as few as they were before their amalgamation in Paris that felt like a lifetime ago.

Mitch sat at a table off to the side of Chandra, and they all waited for her to speak. Slowly, she took a deep breath and spoke up.

"A lot has been asked of you all in this war. We have all sacrificed more than anyone should have to. We have lost good friends, but let us not forget what we are fighting for. Think of your families back home who are saved these horrors because of each and every one of you."

They knew she was building up to something both

important and frightful.

"General Schulz believes that if we were to break the leadership of the enemy, we could drive them from Earth. As the company with the most experience of such matters, he has asked us to fulfil this task."

They sat silently. They were shocked and in disbelief at what they were hearing.

"I will not order any of you to carry out this task, nor will General Schulz. Our intel so far has been solid, and I believe our chance of success to be strong. This will without a doubt be the most dangerous task we have ever undertaken. I cannot promise we will make it back alive, and I cannot promise success."

She paced back and forth while the troops looked on at their leading officer. They were still stunned by what was being asked of them. As eager as they were to get back into action, and have their equipment back, they had never imagined such a task.

"I will not lie to you. Our situation here has become more desperate than ever. The future of our armies in Europe may lie in our hands, and with the task we have been given. We cannot waste any further time in consideration. I must ask you now, whether you will go with me. If you will not, I would ask you to leave the room now. We will not think lesser of you for it. But if you stay, you are in until the very end."

Chandra got no response until Silva stood up and spoke

right at her.

"I think I speak for the Company in saying that we will follow you to the very end, Major."

Grunts of agreement rang out across the lines of troops as they all leapt to their feet, roaring in agreement. Not one of them showed signs of leaving the room. She waved for them to pipe down as Yorath lifted his hand to ask the Major a question.

"Will Major Taylor be joining us, Ma'am?"

"Most certainly. Major Taylor has been fully re-instated. I will be in overall command of the mission that will include a company from the German 13th Mechanised Infantry. My task will be to get us in safely and to manage the mission. Taylor will be responsible for taking care of the enemy leader, known as Karadag, and any of his associates."

"This sounds more like an assassination," said Suarez.

Taylor leapt to his feet.

"You're damn right it is. These bastards don't play fair. They don't abide by any civilised rules of war. It was not so long ago that we faced the threat of a weapon that could eradicate our entire race. We will do anything, and everything, to stop that from happening. If you're not willing to do that, I suggest you hand in your commission and return to civilian life."

Chandra turned and gestured for Taylor to back down. Suarez leaned back in his chair and went silent. He had been made look foolish and cowardly, and it was not for the first time. She had never liked the Lieutenant, but she was also well aware of the fact you can't always have what you want. For all of Suarez's obnoxious attitudes, he was still a useful officer.

"Karadag must die, and whether it is from a nuclear bomb, a precision strike, a gunshot or poison, I couldn't care less. But the outcome will be the same. These aren't humans we are talking about. They might as well be machines, for all I care. I am not going to lose any sleep over the blood I spill of theirs. All I care about is saving as many human lives as possible, including our own."

Suarez dipped his head to look away from the piercing gaze of Taylor. Mitch stepped up beside Chandra and gestured for her to sit down while he continued on.

"The enemy command has been established in the ruins of Paris. In an ideal world, we'd carry out this mission under the cover of darkness just like our other operations in enemy territory. However, this is not an ideal world. A new enemy army is advancing on the defences of Berlin and will likely turn their attention to here when the city falls, and it will."

"A day op, how are we going to make it?"

"I asked the same question myself. Captain Deveron assures me that an Air Force team has been working around the clock to get a few enemy craft operational."

"So we're going to walk right through their defences,

sounds like proper Trojan horse kinda shit," replied Silva.

Taylor smiled. At least they can keep their shit together, he thought.

For the next two hours they outlined the plan and thoroughly relayed the role of everyone in the room. By noon, they were all growing weary of being stuck in the briefing room. The plans were set, and there was little more to do but pray for success. Finally, Taylor stood aside and let Chandra finish up.

"You know the deal, wheels up in one hour! A staging area has been established for us in what used to be landing zone 5b. Ammunition and supplies are awaiting us there. Grab your gear, and make your way there immediately, anymore questions?"

Parker stood up.

"Ma'am, do you really believe this could send their armies packing? That they would leave because we killed the man in charge?"

"I know you have doubts, we all do, but it wouldn't be the first time in history that such a situation has gotten these results. Our experts believe it's possible. I believe it's possible. There are no certainties in this war. All I ask of you all is to put in your all," she replied.

She looked around to see there were many as doubtful as Eli, but they were equally as eager to get to their feet and have something to do. They left in silence. They were glum and deep in thought as they headed to their billets to get their gear. Taylor could see they had the walk of men and women who were expecting to face their death. There was not a lot he could say to quell their fears, for it was a likely possibility.

Taylor was stood in his bedroom assembling his gear when the door swung slowly open, and he turned his head around to see Parker stride through the door. He turned as she leapt into his arms with a kiss. He pulled her back to see the trickle of tears on her face.

"What's happened?" he insisted.

She shook her head as she sobbed and was unable to get out any words. It struck him that it was the most passionate they had been together since before he had been sent to prison. He felt cold inside. Taylor remembered the soothing nights they had spent together, a safe haven from all their troubles. It was a love he had almost forgotten after the despair and misery he had endured.

"We'll make it through this," he whispered.

"Like Friday, Sugar and countless others? I can't lose you, not after everything."

"Hey, we've been through worse."

"Really? Karadag nearly killed you the last time you met, and now you're going to hunt him down?"

"I won't be alone this time. We can do this together."

He hauled her in close and hugged her tightly, hoping it would give some comfort, but he could see there was little chance of that until they had all returned safely. It was understandable, knowing the odds they faced.

"How can we keep doing this? Much more, and there'll be none of us left."

Taylor sighed. He knew how she felt, but he also knew above all they must keep faith.

"And if we aren't fighting and dying, who is? This is what we do. It is what we trained for, what we are paid for, and what we have a duty to do. I want to be with you for the rest of my life, but so does every other loving couple. Most can't make a difference in this war."

She wept further. Eli knew she should remain stronger in the face of all danger, but it was hard to imagine a life without the happiness they had found together.

"In all these years, I never thought I'd find love, and now just when it happens, a wedge is driven between us."

"The only way we can find peace is to end this war. End it for good. We cannot keep fighting this war of attrition. Our mission could end it in one fell swoop, isn't that worth trying for?"

She stepped back and wiped the tears from her face, trying to regain some composure. She didn't like being so weak and helpless, but neither could she hide the feelings she had so recently come to appreciate so dearly.

"I'm gonna kill that bastard, and you're gonna be right there with me when I do!" he stated.

She nodded, but he could see she was far from confident. She hugged him once again, stepped back and turned towards the door. He rushed forward and grabbed her arm. She was hauled around and back into his arms.

"Don't think we aren't going to make it through this. I need you to have faith in me, in all of us. I need you to be the best marine you can be."

Her face grew taut and her posture straightened. She would not let another tear reach her skin. Taylor couldn't tell if she was putting on a brave face for him or genuinely had faith. But at least she won't demoralise the others, he thought. Taylor pulled on his Reitech suit over the German camouflage BDU that still appeared as almost new.

By the time he left the billets, the Company was already streaming towards the landing zone in dribs and drabs. The German Company was already formed up and awaiting their arrival. Their uniforms were well worn, and several displayed recent battlefield cuts and scars, but they all wore brand new Reitech equipment on top. Their leading officer stood before the Company, waiting for Chandra and Taylor. He saluted as they approached.

"Hauptmann... uh Captain Wittman, 391st Mechanised Infantry Battalion."

Chandra stepped up informally to the officer and shook his hand.

"Thank you, Captain. I'm sure you have been fully briefed on your part in this mission?"

"Yes, Ma'am, we ensure the safety of your Company from the surrounding enemy forces. We will have your backs covered."

"You realise what that means, Captain? You'll have the weight of all forces in the area bearing down on you."

"You do what you have to do, Major. We are no strangers to war anymore, and we will do our duty."

The Captain relaxed and smiled as he recognised Mitch.

"Major Taylor, I never thought I would meet you in person. How have you come so far and still be alive?"

Taylor smiled as he shook the hand of the German officer.

"I can't say all my friends have been so lucky."

The two Majors looked down the line of the German Company and could see that they were little more than one hundred and twenty strong.

"You look as if you have seen more than enough action yourselves," added Taylor.

"No, this war is not an experience I would wish on anyone. But it has come down to us."

"Good to have you with us, Captain," replied Chandra. "We'll be loading in five. Good luck, and may we both succeed for the sake of everything and everyone."

The German officer saluted confidently. Chandra already knew he was more than capable of doing what was being asked of him. She gestured for Taylor to follow her to where Captain Jones had assembled their Company. Charlie stood at ease before the troops. He was still doing his job, but the fire in his eyes and the joy in his heart had long gone. He had become so soulless that he was almost a machine.

"Thank you, Captain," shouted Chandra.

It saddened her to see her friend as a shell of the man he used to be. She had looked forward to his return more than anything in their current lives, but she could not help pity the man he now was.

"You all know what we must achieve. Our Generals believe that what we accomplish here could end it all. We cannot fail. We cannot falter, and we cannot stop at any price! Many of us may die here today, but all that matters is that Karadag dies. If we fail, our armies face the biggest threat they have ever known. This mission may likely determine the outcome of the entire war."

She strode along the lines as the troops stood silently awaiting their departure.

"I thank you all for following me into the fire. We have stood together from the very beginning. None of you have faltered. We will fight, and if necessary die together. Good luck to you all. Emplane and prepare for immediate departure!"

"Fall out!" shouted Jones.

The troops rushed towards the three enemy craft that were awaiting them. Few had ever seen the monstrosities up close. Experience had shown they were built as a mixed fighter-bomber that could carry a dozen of the airborne Mechs. The Air Force engineers had stripped out much of the hardware and converted the internals to provide substantial personnel transport bays.

Taylor stepped inside to see Rains at the cockpit, which had been retrofitted at the console as well with as several other human manufactured pieces of equipment.

"Good to see you, Eddie. I thought Schulz would have had your balls by now."

Rains chuckled.

"He saved his wrath for you. I'm just a pilot. I go where I'm posted and do as I'm told."

"You really believe you can get us past their defences in these heaps of junk?"

"I figure so. Those bastards have become wise to our tricks, and they've been identifying my Eagle, despite the modifications. They must be relying heavily on visual identifiers, which is sensible considering."

He tapped his hand on the alien console.

"With these babies, we should glide right in there."

A few minutes later, they were lifting off the landing zone and gaining speed quickly. The engines were almost deafening. The unmistakeable drone of the enemy vessels was something to be feared, and yet they were now travelling aboard the aerial beasts. For all of their raucous bellowing, they were exceptionally fast craft.

The short trip to Paris felt like an afternoon, but they could see through the pilots' cockpit that it was still day. Cloud cover got thicker as they headed further west until they hit rain clouds that peppered the hull. Chandra and Taylor carefully studied the surveillance images on her Mappad one last time.

"They are not a subtle enemy, but they must now know that we are not above these clandestine operations," she whispered.

"You believe they'll be better prepared for us?" asked Taylor.

"I don't know. The weapon in Poitiers was an obvious target that they arrogantly assumed we could not reach. Their leadership may not seem such a draw for us, but they must surely have increased their defences."

"Schulz seemed to think they had little more than fifty Mechs and a similar number of drones in the area."

"Yes, well I wouldn't place too much faith in that."

Taylor smiled.

"We're gonna hit the ground running. Whatever happens, you must find Karadag and end him. I don't care what it costs you. If we all die today alongside that bastard, it will be a mission well done."

"But I pray that not to be our fate."

She nodded in agreement.

"Heads up, we're making our approach!" Rains called out.

Taylor stood up and paced towards the cockpit, gazing out at the enemy base. It had been built right on top of the ruins surrounding the Eiffel Tower. The famous symbol of the city had been smashed during the battle for the city. Taylor could only think that the establishment of the enemy there was intended to rub salt into the wound.

The aircraft rushed over the enemy perimeter defences without opposition. Taylor could make out several dozen enemy Mechs and drones patrolling the grounds as they closed towards a line of metal structures that he recognised from their surveillance images. The buildings were fifty metres high, and their impeccable condition contrasted deeply against the rubble and ruins around them.

The nose of the craft lifted as Eddie came in for a landing. They were putting down in a quiet spot past the nearest structure, and out of the gaze of the patrols further out towards the perimeter. Taylor didn't feel his heart race like he had gotten used to before such dangerous missions. He didn't know if it was because he was used to the emotion, or that he no longer cared for his own life. But as he turned, he saw the faces of Eli, Chandra and the others and remembered why he had feared so much before.

A loud clang rang out as the undercarriage smashed into the ground in a less than eloquent landing. Eddie looked back at them and lifted his hands as if to mutter the word 'what'. It didn't matter. They were on the ground. Sergeant Silva smashed his fist onto the door release button, and it quickly lowered to make a ramp to the surface.

"Here we go again," whispered Taylor.

They rushed out to find an empty and quiet district between the lines of enemy structures. The walls looked as if they were cast from solid steel. A pulsating hum protruded from the area as if some kind of power source was constantly fluctuating up and down. Taylor led the troops out on the ground that was laid with a fresh smooth surface. The enemy had clearly prepared the surface for their base only and left the ruins all around them as trophies of their conquest.

Chandra looked around to see the German Company pouring out from the other two craft. None of the troops wanted to take a step further. No human being could ever want to take a pace closer into the jaws of death, she thought. Taylor looked back and nodded at her in acknowledgement to move forward. She was still in charge overall, but she was more than happy for Mitch to run the Inter-Allied in such a fearful place.

Major Chandra turned to Wittman, pointing for him to split off and head for the perimeter. She hated that she was sending them right for the enemy positions, but it was no different to the dreadful choices she had been making since it all began. She watched as they paced off quickly and quietly to engage the enemy. She turned to see Taylor was already leading the Company forward.

Despite Chandra's discomfort, a tingle went down her spine to see Taylor back among them. It made her feel once again that everything was going to work out. She followed and kept a keen eye on Mitch as he led the advance. Eli Parker was close by his side. As they grew near to the first building, they could hear the heavy footsteps of Mechs steps stomping along a corridor within.

Taylor led them all close along the wall of the structure as he made his way towards what appeared to be the entrance. Ambient lighting, which seemed to emanate from the structures, gave them more than adequate visibility; something they were highly thankful for when they knew they couldn't risk night vision equipment, as gunfire could erupt at any second.

Taylor lifted his hand to stop them and edged forward to get a better view from around the corner of the vast structure. He looked back to check the position of Wittman's troops, but they were already out of sight. He turned back and carefully crept around the corner. He could make out three Mechs stood by the doorway. The sight of them on their own soil reminded him of his encounter with Karadag.

He studied the terrain and spotted two drones a hundred metres away from the guards. He looked back and conveyed the numbers with hand signals before raising his weapon and taking a deep breath. He knew the time for covert action was over. He pointed forward as the go signal and leapt out, rushing towards the doors with his shield held out to protect himself.

He opened fire before the creatures could respond.

BATTLE EARTH III

The first Mech dropped dead when five shots pierced its armour. The drones were quick to respond. They got off several shots, but they were all absorbed by the Reitech shields as the Company advanced. Light from the soldiers' weapons lit up the district as the Mechs and their drones were torn apart. They were still a hundred metres away when the creatures tumbled to the ground in a smouldering heap.

Another two Mechs appeared at the doorway as they approached but were met with a hail of gunfire, riddling each of them with dozens of rounds. Taylor continued at a sprinting pace to the door and slammed into the wall beside the entrance. His platoon formed up around the doorway and prepared to enter. None of them knew what they would find inside, but they were already too pumped up on adrenaline to worry about it.

"Go!" shouted Taylor.

He turned and leapt through the entrance and was the first in. They found themselves in a tall and broad corridor that seemed to continue for as far as they could see. Taylor had expected to see a vast and grand interior but appreciated the cover it afforded them. He looked back to see those who had entered behind him anxiously waiting for the order to continue on. He moved off, knowing they'd be at his back.

He continued on, and they grew closer to the drone from within. Taylor finally reached an adjoining corridor and stepped cautiously to its entrance. He peered around the corner and realised it was as empty as the one they had first entered. He wondered if the enemy had simply not heard the gunfire but knew it was too much to hope for. Chandra pushed her way to the front and stepped up to Taylor.

"Where are they all? Wittman must have made contact by now," she mused.

"With these walls and that noise, there could be all out war, and we wouldn't know it."

"Shit, I don't like this. We don't have a fucking clue where we're going."

Taylor took a deep breath. He knew they had to find Karadag, but he already suspected that the enemy leader would have much the same idea about them.

"Let's keep moving forward," he whispered.

He continued onwards for several hundred metres until they reached an opening. The corridor led into a vast hall that Taylor suspected was at the heart of the structure. Huge towers reached to the roof. It was in this moment that he asked himself, what the hell do they do here? It was a question none had thought to ask when they conceived the mission. The notion that the base was a central hub for Karadag and his leadership was enough.

"What the fuck?" asked Parker.

They continued out into the vast hall and looked in horror as they began to recognise the unmistakeable form of human bodies contained within capsules on the towers. They were inside glass and lined up in columns on the structures.

"My god, there must be thousands of people here," whispered Eli.

"Tens of thousands," replied Chandra.

"What do they want with the bodies?" she asked.

"You're assuming they are dead," replied Taylor.

"They're still alive?" asked Chandra. "Why, and what for?"

"I can think of a few reasons, but none are pleasant," he replied.

He caught a glimmer of movement and squinted to make out half a dozen Mechs that had identified them from across the hall. They were already closing the distance.

"Guess we won't have time to find out!" yelled Taylor.

He leapt aside to the cover of some control module unit as the first light pulses smashed into their location. They had all become more familiar with hiding beneath the enemy fire than they would ever have liked. Taylor peered out from behind the structure and noticed more Mechs pouring into the room.

"We aren't gonna get out of this quick!" he shouted.

Chandra took a look for herself and quickly ducked back into cover as she narrowly evaded an enemy pulse. She sighed, realising they could not afford to stick together, despite the grave danger they faced.

"Take Silva's platoon and find Karadag. We'll take care of this!" Chandra ordered.

Taylor looked into her eyes and wanted nothing more than to disagree, but he had fully accepted there was only one way the mission could end in success. He leapt to his feet, and signalled for the others to follow him and made a quick dash for another corridor. He still had little understanding of where they were going. His information told them that Karadag was inside the complex. He could only hope it was right. Up ahead, the Major could see a door open and Mechs pouring out across the route into another corridor. He turned to Silva.

"We have to stop them, or Chandra's gonna be in the shit."

"Sir, we have a mission to do," he replied.

Captain Jones pushed forward and interrupted.

"Our mission is to kill these fuckers, so let's do it!"

Taylor appreciated the sentiment, but it also concerned him that his friend was so eager to run headlong into danger. Nonetheless, he knew they had to do something.

"Grenades at the ready, let's cut them off!"

He rushed towards the doorway. It was clear that within all the chaos, they had still not noticed the two platoons advancing at their flank. Taylor got within twenty metres when two of the Mechs turned to fire but were riddled with fire and dropped where they stood. He let his rifle hang and pulled two grenades from his webbing and rushed past the door, throwing them in as he did so.

The Major slid across the door opening and lifted his rifle as he reached the other side. Silva and two of the others arrived quickly with him and tossed in grenades from the other side of the frame. The room erupted with an ear-splitting series of explosions, sending vibrations through the walls and floors around them.

Smoke bellowed out from the doorway, but Taylor was quick to his feet and in through the entrance. He fired on full auto from the hip as he engaged the survivors of the room. Several others quickly joined him. For half a minute, they lit up the room with gunfire as they executed the Mechs who were injured, stunned or separated from their weapons.

The room fell silent and the haze seeped away. They could see the bodies of over fifteen Mechs and not a sign of life between them. They couldn't feel any remorse for what they had done, nor anything but satisfaction. Many of the enemy had yet to gather their weapons, when Taylor and the others assaulted them.

"Fuck!" exclaimed Parker.

Taylor looked down to see a puddle of dark blue blood that had streamed across the floor and engulfed one of his boots. He felt repulsed by the sight and only felt his blood lust grow. He lifted his rifle and looked Eli.

"Let's find this bastard."

She looked shocked by the bitter determination in his

face. She hated the alien invaders, but she could not help but feel that a turkey shoot was far from what their duty as soldiers was. Taylor appeared to want only one thing, and at any cost. She prayed he would return to the man she used to know when it was all over, but she was then overcome by the realisation that they had more urgent concerns.

Taylor strode out of the room without a fear in the world. He shot down a passing Mech without breaking stride or raising his shield. He walked like an invincible hero who hunted an inferior being, but none of them wanted to face the creatures' leader who Mitch was so eager to find. The marines quickly followed behind.

Taylor could see a crossroads up ahead. Movement on the opposite corridor, which opened out into the same area, quickly drew his attention.

"Karadag," he spat.

He could recognise the shape of the beast from any distance. Taylor had grown to fear the leader who had almost killed him once, but now he was more driven than ever to rip him apart. He lifted his shield and rifle and quickened his pace. Karadag lifted his right arm and tapped a few commands. Taylor heard a vast blast door smash down behind him. He turned quickly to see one of the marines had been sliced in half by the sheer force. Only Eli and Jones had made it through before the rest of the platoons were cut off.

Taylor stopped and looked at the sight with anger, but he couldn't bring himself to show weakness in the face of the enemy. He turned back to see that Karadag stood awaiting him with a guard either side of him.

"Three on three! Seems a fair fight!" he spat.

Before he could speak another word, he saw Jones leap forward into a sprint.

"Come on, you bastard!" he yelled.

"Jones!" cried Taylor.

It was too late. The Captain had already gained too much speed for them to support him. He fired rapidly on the move, but Karadag skilfully leapt aside. One of the Mechs was struck as it tried to respond to Jones' charge. Charlie didn't break stride and continued to rush for the enemy leader in a furious charge, leaping to barge Karadag with his shield.

The enemy leader moved aside and grasped Jones' shield as he did so. He used his bodyweight and rolled to toss Jones into a nearby wall at high speed. Taylor watched in despair as the alien quickly lifted his stunned friend from the ground and smashed the hilt of his weapon into the Captain's face. Blood sprayed from his head as his body went limp and was tossed aside.

"No!" cried Taylor.

Karadag turned and confidently righted himself from the other side of the room as if to show his physical superiority. Taylor relaxed his shoulders and lifted up from his hunched position. He unclipped his rifle sling and threw down his rifle.

"What are you doing?" yelled Eli.

Taylor didn't respond. He stared at Karadag with a murderous gaze. She could tell that he didn't just want to succeed in their mission. He wanted to make the alien pay. Taylor slowly drew out his assegai and saw the arrogance in the alien's face. He could see that Karadag truly appreciated close combat and that he had no doubt of success against the Major. Eli turned to him in despair.

"You can't do this. He'll kill you," she whispered.

For a moment he ignored her and eyed up his opponent. Karadag turned and gave some signal for his guard to stay put as he advanced slowly and confidently forward. Taylor admired Karadag for his acceptance of single combat, but it didn't stop him hating the creature anymore. He turned back to Eli.

"This is my fight. I came here to end this."

"No, we came here to end this. You can't fight him alone," she pleaded.

"You find a way out of here, Sergeant, and that's an order! I'll finish this, one way or another."

Tears once again streamed from her eyes as she realised Taylor had already accepted that he would die there.

"I told you to go, move!" he yelled.

She lowered her rifle and moved across to the left corridor of the intersection. She looked back one last time to see Taylor and Karadag staring each other down, waiting for the other to make a move. She finally continued onwards and prayed for it all to be over.

* * *

"We're getting fucked here!" yelled Blinker.

Energy pulses smashed into the walls and floor all around their positions as they tried their best to return fire against the increasing Mech forces.

"Just keep firing, Private! We have to give Taylor as much time as we can!" ordered Chandra.

Monty leapt up to take a shot, but as he did, a pulse smashed into his shoulder and threw him back behind the cover. She watched in horror as smoke poured from his body armour, and she could see shards of hot metal burning into the skin of his face. He let out a cry in agony as his brother reached his side, hauling him in against the counter they were using for cover.

"You're okay! You're okay!" he screamed.

He hadn't even looked at the extent of his brother's wounds, but he knew the fact he was breathing was to be considered a rarity after taking a hit from the enemy weapons. He looked down to see that his brother's armour had taken the worst of the impact, but the round had burnt a chunk out of his neck and collar and top of his shoulder.

"Jesus Christ!" cried Blinker.

Chandra wasn't sure if the Private was yelling in concern for his brother or thankful that he had survived the impact. She lifted herself up and continued to fire. She could see yet more Mechs flooding into the vast room, more than they could handle alone.

* * *

Taylor leapt into a sprint and rushed at his opponent. He had seen Karadag's fondness for voiding right against incoming attacks and fully calculated it into his first attack. As he approached with his shield high, the enemy leader rolled just as he had predicted. Taylor dug his heels in and used the power of his suit to re-direct with a quick spin to his left and smashed the shield in Karadag. The alien was caught off balance and tumbled over onto his face.

The remaining guard lifted his weapon to aid his stricken leader, but automatic fire ripped through the intersection and dropped the creature before it could get off a round. Taylor turned to see Eli stood at the corridor entrance with a smoking gun. He smiled in return; she truly was everything he could have ever wanted. As she acknowledged his appreciation, Karadag pulled out a throwing dagger and launched it at the Sergeant.

She responded quickly by lifting her weapon as she spun, and the huge blade embedded in her rifle. She held it up to see that the blade had penetrated right the way through and had come within a few centimetres of her face. She threw the weapon down and glared at the creature with scorn. Taylor watched as Eli drew out her assegai and looked at Karadag with the same contempt and disgust that he shared.

Taylor smiled yet further. He already knew that they were now unstoppable. Parker rushed forward aggressively and leapt towards the beast. Taylor jumped in beside her and thrust forward with his weapon. Karadag frantically cut across his body and parried the two weapons and spun with a hard swing against Taylor. He lifted his shield at the last moment, and the huge two-handed blade crashed into the thick metal.

Mitch felt the impact through his entire body and was only thankful that the exoskeleton suit saved his body from crumpling. The impact had carved a deep groove into the shield with a channelled dent that surrounded it. Taylor could already tell that it had buckled. He pushed upwards with the shield and drove his sword up towards the beast's torso.

Karadag kicked the Major's arm aside and lifted to make a heavy vertical stride that would have smashed Taylor to the ground, but was interrupted by Eli. She jumped forward and hit Karadag with all her force behind the shield that sent him staggering back. She knew that such a strike would have killed a human being, but it only appeared to make him angrier.

The two marines stood awaiting their enemy's next move, but he circled them and cautiously tried to search out their weaknesses.

"Major Taylor, why will you not just die?" he growled.

The deep booming voice echoed around the huge empty crossroads.

"I might well ask you the same question. We never wanted this war. We never came looking for you. Look what you have done. You want to systematically erase our species!"

"Yeeeeesss..." he replied.

Eli shook her head in disgust. He was proud of the fact.

"What are you doing with all these people here? Thousands of them..." she replied.

Karadag turned and looked down at her as if she was a lesser being, although it amused him to sicken her further with an answer.

"Those suitable are being re-programmed. They should make adequate soldiers in our armies."

"What, humans? They'll never fight for you!" she spat back.

Karadag let out a slow, deep bellowing laugh that was meant to insult her as much as it was for his own entertainment.

"Humans? All these thousands of years, and look how little distance you have come."

"We seem to be kicking your ass well enough," replied Taylor.

Karadag's eyes lit up a fiery red as he screamed out and swung his huge weapon down against the Major. It was a careless and uncontrolled strike that he easily avoided, thrusting his assegai into the beast's arm. Karadag gave out a short scream in pain before kicking Taylor in the chest and launching him across the room. He then turned his attention back on Eli as Taylor sighed in pain, trying to get some air back into his lungs.

"A woman in your army? Is that how little understanding you have? You accept weakness?"

She leapt and used her boosters to launch her into the air as she screamed and thrust for Karadag's face. He parried it aside, but she continued the assault with a barrage of attacks as she descended. In her wild frenzy, she left herself open, and Karadag thrust the back shaft of his two-hander into her stomach, throwing her back. She tumbled along the floor until she came to a stop just two metres from where Taylor was struggling to get to his feet.

The two marines got up together and looked into each others' eyes. It was in this moment that Taylor realised he didn't want to die there. He nodded to Eli, and she could already see his thoughts.

"Let's do this," he stated.

They both turned and strode in time towards the

arrogant alien leader. Parker parried his first strike as Taylor attacked, and they for the first time fought in harmony. Karadag could barely respond in time to the flurry of attacks, and they could see the worry in his eyes. In a panicked attacked, he cut down with all his force against Eli, but she parried with both hands supporting her shield. Taylor leapt forward and smashed the bottom edge of his shield onto Karadag's leading knee.

The creature's leg buckled under the power of the blow, and he fell down onto the injured joint. Eli jumped forward and thrust her assegai into his stomach. The brutal weapon pierced his armour without any resistance. His head lifted, and his jaw opened as he let out a screech in pain. He looked back down and lifted his weapon to try and strike, but Taylor thrust forward also.

Parker and Taylor pulled out their swords and continued to stab Karadag repeatedly as he dropped his sword, and they saw the energy in his eyes fade. He collapsed down heavily on the hard floor as pools of blood spread all around him. Eli breathed a sigh of relief, but Taylor paced forward and knelt down beside the head of the dying leader. Karadag spluttered as he tried to speak a few words.

"It isn't over, it's never over..."

His voice faded, and his head slumped. Neither of them was in doubt that he was dead. Taylor turned to see Parker leap onto him with a hug.

"We did it!" she cried.

He pulled her back to see her body armour was badly battered from the fight, but that she was okay. She wiped the blood from his face, and he winced at the pressure on his broken nose and bruised face.

"Remind me I never want to go into boxing," he jested.

She smiled as tears streamed down her face.

"Let's get the hell out of here."

* * *

Chandra looked at Blinker with a look of surprise as she heard a volley of weapons fire in the distance that she knew not to be of enemy origin. She leapt up to see friendly troops engaging the Mechs from the far corridor where they had come from.

"It's Wittman!" she cried.

The soldiers who had been huddled behind cover jumped to their firing positions with a newly found confidence. Having others come to their aid was something the Inter-Allied were beginning to forget. They leapt out from cover and advanced on the Mechs, firing as they did so. Chandra turned to see that Eli had joined in from a side corridor, and she could make out the shape of Taylor firing one-handed and with a fellow soldier over his shoulder.

The human forces closed quickly on the Mech forces and with continued fire quickly overcame them. Chandra turned in surprise to see Jones slung over Taylor's shoulder, and the damage they had all taken.

"Is it done?" she asked.

Taylor grinned in such a way that she already knew the answer.

"Then what are you waiting for? Get your arses out of here!"

She turned to Wittman and the others.

"We've got minutes until the enemy descend upon us, and we're done for. Let's move it!"

They quickly got up to pace and followed the route they had come in. She rushed up beside Jones.

"Mitch, is he alive?" asked Chandra.

"I think he'll make it! Next time he wants to commit suicide, he can do it on your watch!"

She looked over in despair at the unconscious body of the Captain who both of them had come to know as a great friend. He was a casualty of war that wasn't reflected in the casualty reports. They rushed out of the vast building to find little more than a scattering of Mechs and drones that opened fire. One of Silva's platoon was hit and killed, but the rest quickly returned fire without breaking pace.

Campbell hauled the body of the fallen soldier onto his shoulders. Now knowing what they did, they could never leave a comrade behind, no matter the stakes. The exhausted Taylor rushed to the front of the troops even with the weight of Jones on his shoulders. He wanted nothing more than to get free of the enemy lines.

The two Companies poured aboard the three craft while under continuous fire by the oncoming Mechs. They could tell the enemy was far from ready for the lightning strike they had made, and now there was little available to stop them escaping.

"Eddie! Get is the fuck out of here!" yelled Taylor.

The ramps were still lifting as the craft took off. Several pulses smashed into the craft Rains was piloting, but they did little more than shake the vessel. After getting just thirty metres off the ground, Eddie put all power to the rear engines and soared to full speed. They all knew once they had reached full speed that nothing the enemy had could catch them.

"Jesus Christ, Major, you trying to get me killed?" asked Eddie.

"Mighty fine job you did here, Lieutenant. I'll be sure to make the General aware of your work."

"Fuck that, you keep me alive and get me a beer, and I'll be good."

Taylor smiled. He stepped back into the transport bay and looked down in sadness at the body of the fallen soldier. He noticed Monty and knelt down beside the man.

"Some good wounds to brag about back home there?"

"Yes, Sir," he responded with gritted teeth.

Taylor patted him on his good shoulder.

"Damn fine soldiering, Monty."

They arrived back on base within hours to a hail of applause by an entire division that had assembled to greet them, along with detachments from a dozen countries. When they hit the ground and disembarked, Chandra could see that Wittman had over a dozen dead and almost as many wounded. It saddened her to see what a price it had cost them, but they were welcomed back as heroes, nonetheless.

General Schulz and his staff awaited them and saluted as they paced down the ramps. Taylor smirked as he was amused by the amount of kiss ass he knew he had earned from the man who had sent him to prison. Though he looked past to Dupont who still glared at him with disgust and refused to salute.

"Major Chandra, Major Taylor, welcome back!"

They could see the General was desperately awaiting news. They could have transmitted it soon after breaking free of the enemy blocking zone, but they were less than eager to send the news ahead and let their superiors take the glory. Schulz lifted up his hand for the troops to silence themselves and listen to Chandra. He beckoned for his aide to go forward with a microphone that had been linked to speakers all around the base.

"Major, please tell us the news."

"Thank you, General, but I must let Major Taylor have this duty, for he has earned it more than any of us."

Schulz begrudgingly accepted. She could see that his

hatred of Taylor had waned to little more than a mild annoyance, but it still pained him to see Taylor stealing the spotlight. She passed the mic to Taylor who coughed to clear his throat. He looked out at the eager faces of all the soldiers who awaited the news. Line after line of troops watched him with eager eyes; so many faces that reminded him of all those they had lost on the road to this point.

"I can confirm that as of 1500 hours today, Karadag, the leader of the enemy army on Earth, is dead, witnessed by myself and Sergeant Eli Parker of the 2nd Inter-Allied Battalion..."

The roar of clapping and whistles cut off his speech as the troops could not restrain themselves. They could hear the celebrations ring out across the base. There was not one among them who could not leap for joy at the news. After several minutes of ecstasy, they finally quietened and waited for him to continue.

"We did this together, not as a nation, an army, but as a race. We stood together as the human race. I can guarantee you that this war is not over, but I can also assure you that I will not stop fighting until it is!"

General Schulz stepped forward and raised his hand to ask Taylor for the microphone. He handed it over without question. He didn't like the man, but he liked speaking publically even less. Schulz picked up the mic and turned back to the troops with a smile.

"This is General Schulz, Commander of the joint

European armies. I want to thank you all for your continuing efforts. We believe that our actions today have broken the spine of this invading force. I have already had confirmation that Russian, Swedish and Danish troops are already well on their way to assisting in the Battle for Berlin. That fight is no longer our concern."

He stopped for a moment and took a deep breath for dramatic effect.

"We can drive our enemy into the sea, and I fully intend to do it. At 0500 hours we advance east, and we keep advancing until we reach the sea!"

* * *

One week later. Taylor and Chandra stood at the foot of Jones' hospital bed. His body was all but recovered, but he gazed into space without any sense of reality.

"Charlie, France is saved. Tartaros is leaving!" shouted Chandra in joy.

He looked over at her with a blank expression. A few months previously it would have been the greatest news the Captain could ever have heard, but now it was if it went in one ear and out the other. The doors swung open, and Taylor turned quickly to see Sergeant Dubois stood before them and gazing at the Captain with sorrow.

"May I?" she asked.

Taylor nodded and took a pace back to let her pass

and stand at his bedside. She knelt down beside the bed so that her eyes were at his level. She said nothing, only staring back into his eyes and deep into his soul. She did so for what felt uncomfortably long. Finally, she stretched forward and kissed the Captain.

Taylor watched in amazement as his eyes flickered, and for a moment he saw the life return to them. He reached out and laid his arms around the French woman, holding her tightly. From over her shoulder, he turned and nodded to Taylor; a recognition that Mitch had not seen since they had returned from Paris. Chandra smiled as she realised that Dubois might well have brought him back from the brink of insanity with a single kiss.

Taylor turned to Chandra.

"This isn't over. We have broken the enemy's will to fight, but there will be more leaders, more armies. Can you honestly believe whatever other forces they have could let us get away with this?"

Chandra shrugged her shoulders. She wanted to celebrate the victory they had and worry about the future a different day.

"Come on, let's leave them to it."

They stepped out to find, much to their surprise, General Schulz sat in the waiting room for them with several members of his staff.

"How is Captain Jones?" he asked.

Taylor strolled up to the General and could see the

concern in his eyes was genuine. For the first time since they had met, he did not hate the man.

"I believe he may have a chance," replied Taylor.

"That's wonderful news. The war is over, and the enemy is in full retreat."

"To where?" he responded.

"Where, why should we care? Anywhere, but here!"

Taylor nodded in appreciation of the news, but he was far from wholly satisfied. He looked past the General to one of his aides.

"Get a message to the Moon for me."

"Uhh..."

Schulz turned around and nodded in agreement to the young officer.

"A message from me, Major Taylor, to Commander Kelly of the Moon Defence Force. Tell him the war isn't over. Tell him, we're coming for him. We're coming to take back all our lands, human lands."

He turned back to Schulz.

"Earth has been saved, but while the enemy values our planet and know our location, this war will never be over..."

BATTLE EARTH III